THE SHIMMER

ALAIN BOULANGER was born in France and migrated to Australia as a child and eventually settled in Hong Kong. He is the illustrator and editor of the children's book *John The Fish and Other Stories*. This is his first novel.

THE SHIMMER

THE SHIMMER

ZODIAC BOOKS

for
Eden and Adam,
never stop dreaming.

THE SHIMMER

CHAPTER 1

Jarod Johnson had a problem.

It had only been two weeks, but it was getting increasingly annoying. For someone who spent his days at a computer terminal working as an IT project manager in the credit cards department of a major bank in Hong Kong, he found concentrating on his job increasingly difficult. At the age of forty-two, he had been working for the firm nearly twenty years now, too long by anyone's standard. But the security of a regular salary kept him at his desk for all those years and paid the mortgage.

He slid back on his black office chair, his thin but toned frame somewhat at odds with the rest of the room. His brown hair was cropped, his nose straight and strong, and his tan indicated he loved the outdoors. He wore blue slacks with a white shirt opened at the collar and a red tie.

He looked at the flat screen in front of him and tried hard to focus on his task. The blue glow and white fonts were as familiar to him as the fingers on his right hand.

There it was again.

It was barely distinguishable at the corner of his right eye, almost like a heat wave rising from the macadam on a scorching summer day.

But this was worse.

It was not a hot summer day, and Jarod was not lost in the middle of a desert. He was cocooned inside his blue five-by-five cubicle. The air conditioning in the building was set at 71 degrees, too cold for his comfort. At times, he felt a pressure at the back of his neck, like a cold hand forcing him down on his chair.

It was there and had been there for the last couple of weeks. Right at the corner of his right eye, almost outside his field of vision, but as real and infuriating as a mosquito flying around his head.

Jarod closed his eyes.

Maybe it would make it go away.

But even with his eyes closed, he could still see *it* like a constant itch, which, no matter how hard you scratched, wouldn't disappear.

Barely visible but there nonetheless.

He opened his eyes and tried to re-focus on his work.

But it was in vain.

The Functional Specification document staring lifelessly back at him was a blur in comparison to the unceasing, hardly discernible shimmering wave of light.

All around him he could hear the soft click of thousands of keystrokes, which defined and shaped the technology of the world he lived in. Not another sound could be heard except for the occasional whisper during a phone call, as if the operator was afraid of breaking the monotonous hum of the air conditioning system.

This place was depressing. It smelled of plastic, paper and aftershave. It smelled like an alternative life, like those white characters all over the blue screen in front of him—suffocating and dull.

Jarod looked around him; a beehive with all the worker bees sitting in their individual alcoves working their asses off.

For what?

He sat high on his chair so as to keep an eye on his asshole boss, who had a tendency to sneak up on him. She was some twenty pounds overweight, wore too much make-up and dressed like a man.

But she managed to sneak behind him before he had time to notice. "How are things going, Jarod?"

"Good."

"Anything to report?"

"Nope."

"All on track?"

"Yep."

"Good to hear. Keep at it."

God, he hated the bitch, and he hated his job. How did he ever get stuck here, in this dead-end piece of shit job? Life was a sick joke for him and everyone else in this office. They are all going to die one day, and this was as good as it gets.

He looked around again.

10:47 a.m.

Two rows to his left, he could see a head with blond hair bobbing up and down like a float with a fish at the end of its hook. His friend Peter Smith was enjoying an early morning snooze.

Peter was great, though. He did work pretty hard when he was in the mood—guess he wasn't in the mood right now.

Jarod had met Peter twelve years ago and they had become best friends. Both sport freaks, they would find any excuses to be outdoors rather than stuck in the office. They spent almost every lunchtime together and hated team lunches which, somehow, they mostly always managed to escape from. After a few no-shows, the Credit Card team finally got the hint and stopped bugging them.

Work was just work, and they found happiness over a fag on the second floor of the parking lot—a quiet moment among exhaust fumes and the screeching of tires moving beyond the 5 km/hr speed limit.

Those five minutes, the length of a fag, were the little highlight of their endless, boring, yet so hectic day. They caught up on gossip and surrendered themselves to the guilty pleasure of nicotine hitting their central nervous system.

On that usual Tuesday morning Jarod told Peter his problem. He took a deep, initial, satisfying drag of his first cigarette of the day.

"Buddy," he said and pointed at his right eye, "do you see something wrong with my right eye?"

"Well yeah, of course," Peter said, pretending to examine Jarod's eye. "To start with, they're green and not blue like mine, so that sucks."

"Ha ha, funny. Seriously dude, I feel like... it's hard to explain. There is a shimmer on my right field of vision, like, you know when its really hot and the heat rises from the ground?"

"Right, and—"

"—well, it's at the corner of my right eye, and it's driving me up the wall!" He took another drag of cigarette. "It's been annoying me for two weeks, on and off. Even when I close my eyes, I can still see it." He felt the butt's consumed end searing the tip of his fingers and flicked it, not caring where it landed. "I don't know what the hell is wrong with me, and it's scaring me. I mean, I'm not going blind or something, am I?"

Peter took a deep drag from his cigarette and reflected on his friend's problem. "Listen," he finally said, "it's probably nothing. I mean you're staring at a computer terminal all day, so of course your eyes are going to be a little screwed. It's probably normal, and—"

"—but it's not happening to you now, is it?" Jarod said, a little too much anger in his tone.

"Okay, okay, don't get your knickers in a knot." Peter gave his cigarette one last flick. "Maybe it's because your eyes are fucked-up green while mine are a ravishing blue. Hey, I don't know, have you been to see an optometrist or something?"

"Well," Jarod said, "I was hoping it would go away by itself, but it's getting worse everyday."

"Go and see a doctor."

"Actually, I'm kinda worried going to the doc. I'm scared he's gonna tell me something I don't wanna hear. Like, dude, you're fucked and you gonna spend the rest of your already fucked-up life walking around with a white fucking cane, and hitting every fucking tree just going to 7-11 for a fucking carton of milk. Mate I'm screwed! Fuck! What am I gonna do?"

It was obvious to Jarod Peter felt sorry and worried about his best friend. Life did suck in a way but *this* would suck major. Peter tried to sound nonchalant in order to make Jarod feel better.

"Relax, its probably nothing. I mean it doesn't have to mean you're going blind or anything. It's probably just an abnormality in your eye. Go and see a specialist, and you'll feel much better."

"Are you sure?" Jarod said.

"Dude, this is me you're taking to. In fact, I know a good eye specialist. His name is Andrew So. His office is in Kowloon. I'll give you his contact when we get back to the office, okay? And talk about getting back, lets get out asses into gear. I have a meeting five minutes ago."

CHAPTER 2

"**Hi** babe!" Jarod said as he entered the one-bedroom apartment he shared with his girlfriend Catalina Ling. She was a stunner and wasn't afraid to show it. Her large, almost black, almond shaped eyes and her long silky black hair drove him crazy.

She had high-cheeked bones, a well-defined jaw, and a long, slender neck. Her breasts were small yet firm, just the way he liked them. She was a dream girl, and Jarod often wondered how such a hot girl could be in love with a bum like him.

She loved the aerobics classes with her friend Sophie, her coffee black and strong without a hint of sugar—telling Jarod she was sweet enough—and her job as an Event Manager at the Mandarin Oriental Hotel.

And it wasn't just her looks that turned Jarod on. She was also incredibly smart and had a great personality. Her life was perfect and she was totally in love with Jarod.

They had only met three months earlier and had decided to move in together. He knew she loved his slim, muscular frame and the way he always made sure her orgasms were his first priority in bed.

"Hi JJ babe," she said, her voice echoing in the confinement of the small apartment. "How was your day, honey?"

"Oh, okay I guess." He removed his tie and threw it on the red couch. "Just the same as every other day. Nothing special, you know."

"Well, mine was great." Her voice was coming from the bathroom. The door had been left ajar. She never closed it, and Jarod wondered if she did it on purpose for him to take a peek. There was a naughty side to her, and he liked it.

In fact, he was now thinking of the time they had met on that cool autumn night. The IFC rooftop bar. The one too many drinks, and then, the icing on the cake—the invitation to go back to her apartment for a cup of coffee. The oldest trick in the book. And of course, he didn't have to be asked twice.

As he had been following her up the two flights of stairs to her apartment, he had walked as closely behind her as he had dared without seeming to be a predator. He could smell her floral perfume, but underneath his nostrils detected a hint of her musky odor evading her slightly perspiring skin, making his animal instincts come alive and giving him an illusion, if not wishful thinking, of her eagerness to mate with him.

The stairway had been dark and narrow and the stirring in his loins had become increasingly noticeable.

"Can you turn on the kettle while I take a quick shower?" she had said.

Her apartment was small and messy. It had a female scent. A mixture of perfumes sprayed on hastily as she rushed out the door everyday. Always late, he imagined.

On the coffee table had sat an unwashed cup with the words *Good Morning Sex*, and a small plate with bread crumbs still left over from that morning's breakfast. Jarod had taken the cup and plate to the kitchen sink and had just been about to wash them when he had heard the shower being turned on.

Looking in the direction of the bathroom, he had seen the light streaming from the half opened door. He could imagine her, standing there naked with the hot water streaming down the full length of her body.

He had walked towards the light in a hypnotic state. The stirring in his pants had now become almost unbearable.

He had pushed the door open—just an inch. The hot steam had slowly escaped and dissipated like mist on a mountain top as the morning sun shines upon it. Her ghostly figure had started to fade and in instead, the shape her body had begun to emerge and reveal itself. As the smog had finally dissipated, she has finally been there in all her splendor and breathtaking beauty—the long black hair flowing all the way down to the small of her back. Her buttocks round and firm and her long, her so very long, beautifully shaped legs. The smell of peach shampoo had risen to his nose and his nostrils had flared in an attempt to inhale more of her.

At the sound of his approach, her head had slowly turned and he could see the tendons of her long neck straining so her eyes would meet his. He had seen her inviting smile. She knew he would come in, she knew he wouldn't be able to resist the *cup of coffee*. She knew him so well, even back then.

Snapping back into reality, he looked around. The room was messy as usual, the white silk panties on the floor, as usual. And of course, the ajar bathroom door and the smell of her perfume were also there to welcome him.

Everyday he would come home, and no matter how bad his day had been, that bathroom door would always excite him and make him forget, for a while anyway, the crazy routine his working life had become.

Jarod walked to the bar and poured himself a glass of whiskey.

The shower stopped.

The warm and smooth whiskey slowly ran down his throat and helped sooth his concerns. The sweet phenolic taste and ethanolic aroma were as good to him as sex—well almost.

"Hello there," Catalina said, "Anybody home?"

"Oh sorry, babe," he mumbled as he came out of his

hypnotic state. "I was just preoccupied with something I had to do at the office."

"JJ babe, it's just work." Her voice was still coming from the bathroom, and he saw her in his mind's eye totally naked. "Let it go. Whatever it is, it will still be there tomorrow. So worrying is not going to change anything."

"Yes, you're right," he said and took a sip and felt the warmth in his tummy. "How was your day?"

"As I was telling you, great," she said and stepped out of the bathroom in a silk negligee, so transparent she might as well have been wearing rice paper.

Jarod couldn't help but stare and was still wondering how he, of all people, had ended up with someone as beautiful as Catalina.

She smiled mischievously and said, "How is your whiskey? Can I have one?" She sneaked closer, like a predator circling its prey. "And, while you're there, you can stop dribbling."

"Ha ha," Jarod said nervously and poured a double dose into her favorite glass. "You got me there..."

"I can read your like an open book, mister. I know exactly what you want." She grabbed the whiskey and in one gracious, seamless move rose one long shapely leg and sat on top of him.

Jarod could smell her. So close, so sensual. He just couldn't get enough of her. Everyday he reminded himself that no matter how bad his day had been, there was always something, or rather someone amazing waiting for him as he stepped into his private kingdom, his castle, his paradise.

He saw her small Adam's apple move up and down as she took a sip of her drink.

The whiskey was making him lightheaded and warm inside. Slowly her hips swayed from side to side like a boat on the surface of the ocean.

She looked into his eyes, and it felt as if she could read his innermost thoughts.

She pressed her lips against his. They were filled with passion and the warm taste of whiskey.

He closed his eyes and he drowned in a sea of tranquility and effortlessness.

He sank deeper and deeper.

But something was wrong.

He could feel it.

As subtle as a feather against this cheek, *it* was there. Right there.

No, please! Not now, please!

He jerked up and the glass fell out of his hand and shattered on the tiled floor.

"JJ! What's wrong with you?" she said as she nearly fell off his lap. "Are you okay?"

The moment was gone.

Her eyes were wide open, her face in a state of stupor and fear, the whiskey all over her negligee.

The shimmer had returned.

His eyes tried to catch it, but all he could see was the bar fridge in a wavering, mirage-like appearance.

Catalina got up. She looked worried and annoyed. This had already happened more than once—the sudden jerk. It always seemed to happen when things were going so well, somehow always spoiling the moment.

She had been patient with him, but now it looked as if she had had enough. He could tell she was trying to remain calm, but the tone of her voice was strained. "Is it that, whatever you call it, shimmer again?"

"I'm sorry, babe," Jarod said, feeling like an idiot. The shimmer had already vanished as mysteriously as it had appeared. "I am truly sorry." he tried again, attempting to sooth her. "It's always the same but it seems to be getting worse."

She was now back on the couch with her legs crossed and the whiskey on the coffee table. The seductiveness had gone out of her voice. "You should really go and see a doctor."

"I will. I promise. In fact, Peter gave me the number of an optometrist. I'll see him first thing tomorrow."

She smiled and uncrossed her legs. "Okay, honey. Just relax. Let me give you a massage and see where it might lead."

Jarod laid back on the couch.

He closed his eyes and tried to relax.

The shimmer was gone.

For now anyway.

CHAPTER 3

"**A**lright, Mr. Johnson, now I'm going to squeeze in a couple of drops in order to check your eye pressure, and then we are going to check the back of your eyes."

The optometrist, Dr Andrew So, was tall and thin. His skin was pale, most likely from the long hours he spent indoors, not getting much vitamin D. His Asian features resembled those of a mole, which had spent its life underground sniffing for worms. His hands were thin with prominent blue veins. His fingers were long and his nails manicured to a perfect crescent shaped moon.

Jarod hated being a patient. He hated being manipulated and analyzed like an experimental lab rat.

He looked around. Why did examination rooms always look so intimidating?

"Okay, here we go. Now keep your eyes open and do not move," Dr So said.

Easy for him to say, you try to have something pocking into your eye and see if you can sit still.

But the pressure wasn't that bad, and Jarod thought he ought to stop being a wuss.

"Well, no problem here," Dr So said. "Now let's check the

back of your eyes and look out for diabetes, high blood pressure, muscular degeneration, retina detachment, glaucoma and so on. You'd be amazed what we can find out just by examining the back of the eyes, Mr. Johnson."

"Okay, but what about the shimmer I told you about? Is that gonna help?"

"Let's just see what we detect for now, and then we'll conduct further tests if these don't provide us with the information we need. Please stand still and look straight ahead."

Jarod felt a slight pressure as Dr So examined the back of his eyes but nothing too uncomfortable. This wasn't so bad after all. Maybe optometrists were not as scary as dentists. They don't drill or pull your eyes out like dentists drill and pull your teeth out.

"Right, done." Dr So said and rolled back on his stool from the ophthalmic stand. He made his way back to his computer terminal. "Okay, stay still for a couple of minutes." Dr So's eyes were glued to the screen. "Since your pupils are dilated, they will let in more light, and your vision will remain blurry for the next two to three hours. After we're done, I suggest you go home and rest until your vision is back to normal."

Jonathan couldn't see anything and rubbed his eyes with the back of his hand. The light entering his now gigantic pupils felt like he was being interrogated with a spotlight pointed directly at his face. He blinked a few times and felt tears running down his face. He used the tissue the optometrist had given him to wipe them away.

"Thank you," he said, embarrassed at how his voice sounded like he had been crying. He shook his head and his voice became normal again. "Have you found anything to explain the shimmer?"

"You eyes are fine, Mr. Johnson." Dr So swiveled on his chair to face him. "The symptoms you have seem like the onset of a migraine, but you have been telling me that you only have had minor headaches. There is most likely nothing wrong with your eyes. I have seen a couple of cases like yours and it's probably neurological. It's the part of your brains controlling your vision that's malfunctioning, and this is what's probably causing the shimmer you've experienced." Dr So rolled his chair closer. "It's nothing to worry about. We can conduct further tests, but I don't think it will achieve anything."

This optometrist isn't helpful.

"You're telling me there is nothing wrong with my eyes and it's all in my head?" Jarod stood up and faced the optometrist from a higher vantage point. There was no way he was going to walk out of this office without further explanation. "Come on, doc, this is driving me crazy! And it's happening almost everyday now."

Spittle landed on the doctor's neat white lab coat.

Jarod knew he had gone going a bit far but he didn't care. "It's really driving me nuts. What the hell am I suppose to do?"

Dr So was taken aback. He stood up and stepped away from Jarod. It was rare for a patient to lose it during an eye examination. "Calm down, Mr. Johnson. I can understand how upsetting this is and I will do my best to find out the cause. I can assure you it is not your eyes that are causing the shimmer, but something in your brain." He sat down in an attempt to diffuse the tension. "In the meantime, I will recommend you to a neurologist. What you have could be the beginning of something called multiple sclerosis, where your immune system goes into overdrive, gets confused and starts attacking healthy tissues in your body, including the optic nerves."

Jarod was only half listening. He felt like he was in a trance.

Ten minutes later, outside the building, his vision was still blurry from the eye drops. Everything looked surreal. As if the shimmer wasn't bad enough, now he had to put up with dilated pupils and the resulting blinding light.

Is this what his vision would permanently become? This veil, constantly there, this annoying shimmer screwing up his life. He knew Catalina had been patient, but her patience could only go so far. Sooner or later she'd have enough and leave him. He'd most likely would leave her eventually if the roles were reversed.

Lost in his own thoughts, he almost tripped over an old woman sitting on the ground, her legs blocking half the pedestrian walk.

Jarod's eyes leveled with hers.

She was old. Very old. Wrinkles lined her face like the severely cracked soil of a desert that hadn't seen rain for a hundred years. The eyes had formed cataracts that veiled them as if her light brown irises were trying to hide behind the milky substance. Her hair, gray and streaked with white, was pulled back into a bun too tight and seemed to want to stretch the skin around her temple to make her brow seem smoother. Her tiny nose was like a button. Her cracked lips framed crooked yellow teeth held together by a single wire with gaps wide enough to leave little to the imagination as to the inside of her mouth. Her clothes were ragged but clean. Everything she wore was black or gray, as if all the colors had been drained from her presence—as if she was but a hundred year old photograph.

Her cardigan was moth-eaten in several places, and the black trousers she was wearing were held together by a length of cord coiled around her thin frame. To her left sat an old cookie steel box that looked like it hadn't seen a crumb in fifty years. A few coins were sitting inside it.

Jarod was always hesitant in giving money to beggars. But somehow, this old woman seemed to stir something within him. The thought of his own mother—she was old, lonely, but comfortable in her own home. He dug into his pocket and tossed a few coins into the tin box.

And that's when he noticed the young, Asian girl sitting

next to the old woman. The school uniform she wore was loose on her bony frame. It reminded Jarod of a scarecrow. Her hair was dark and tangled in a disarray that made the roots of a banyan tree look neat. It fell upon her frail shoulders, almost covering them like a cape. She wore a pair of plastic, black-framed glasses too big for her small face. Jarod also noticed a small thin scar running from her bottom lip to the corner of her chin. It wasn't unattractive and gave her a look of toughness and independence, even at her young age.

Almost as if on cue, the girl looked up. Not to the left or right, but straight into Jarod's eyes. The thick smeared lenses of her glasses did nothing to hide her eyes. Those dark brown eyes, almost too large for her oriental features, reached out to him. He tried to turn away, but she kept on staring.

Then suddenly, she smiled, showing a set of small, neat, white teeth. "Hello sir," she said in a tiny, almost indiscernible mousy voice.

"Hi there," Jarod said, unable to look away. "What's your name?"

"Mary Xun. And you, sir?"

"I'm Jarod."

The verbal exchange made him fell a little more comfortable.

"Nice to meet you, sir," Mary said without breaking her sweet smile.

Jarod felt a sense of déjà-vu but this was not possible since he had never met the young girl. Maybe he had passed the old woman before, and the girl had been there, and he never really noticed her, but his sub-conscious did? The sense of déjà-vu was so strong though, it felt as if they had really met in another life.

"What are your doing here, Mary? Are you helping this old woman?"

"Oh no, sir. This my grandmother. I finish school for the day, so I bring her rice to eat."

"Your grandmother?" Jarod said, unable to hide the shock on his face. "Why is she begging in the streets? Where are your parents?"

Mary stood up and took a step towards Jarod.

Jarod noticed that a couple of people had stopped to look at them. He guessed it wasn't very often they saw a foreigner talking to a schoolgirl. He worried they might think he was some kind of pedophile.

"My mum and dad died in car accident two years before," the schoolgirl said. "Then just me and Pawpaw and not have more money so Pawpaw sit all day and get more money."

"Oh, I'm sorry to hear that, Mary. Can't anyone help you and Pawpaw? You don't have any other family members?"

Mary stepped forward, now very close to Jarod. He felt uncomfortable with people looking at them.

Her liquid black eyes looked up at him. "We get money from government, but is not enough. So Pawpaw need sit and ask for more money. School expensive so need more money."

Jarod was flabbergasted. It was crazy how in this day and age an old woman and her grandchild had to live in such conditions—beg in order to make ends meet.

He massaged the back of his neck and said, "So, it's just you and her."

"Yes, sir, just me and Pawpaw." She looked down at her grandmother and smiled. "But she nice and she take care of me and I take care of Pawpaw." Her eyes fell back on Jarod. "We have little money, but we happy together."

Jarod couldn't help but feel sorry for Mary and her grandmother. It's something he never really thought about. He lived his life, and he had his own problems and never had time to look around him. The poverty, the misery, the struggle— what some people had to go through just to survive, just to have a meal on their plates.

He took twenty dollars out of his wallet and placed it into Pawpaw's bony hand. He saw her face lighten up like a candle,

17

and an almost toothless smile emerged from her wrinkled face.

Jarod smiled and turned back to Mary. "What's your grandmother's name, Mary?"

Mary looked at Pawpaw tenderly. "Xun Li Suen," she said.

Upon hearing her name, Pawpaw looked up at Jarod. She extended her claw-like hand, which Jarod took into his. It felt like a dry branch, and he was scared to crush it.

She smiled. An impossible amount of wrinkles lined her prune-like face. "Nit to mit you," she said.

"And nice to meet you, too," Jarod said and smiled in return. He carefully shook her hand.

He looked around him, but no people were no longer looking at them. He assumed they must have gotten bored with the scene and had decided to move on.

He turned back to Mary. "Where do you and Pawpaw live? Do you have a place to stay?"

Mary bit her lip, and her smile disappeared. "Yes, sir. Pawpaw and I live in Sheung Sha Wan. It very old and it very small." Her smile came back as quickly as it had vanished. "But me guess is okay for just me and Pawpaw."

Jarod was thinking fast now. He could still feel this special bond with Mary. He didn't know why, but he knew he had to see her again. He thought of doing more to help them. Maybe he could give them some money. But why them? What was it that made him feel like he just couldn't leave and never look back? He felt a connection—he couldn't leave it at that.

He took a step closer to Mary. "I want to help you and Pawpaw if you would allow me to do so," he said without a second thought.

Mary looked into his eyes again. Maybe she could also feel the connection. There was surprise and a bit of fear in the darkness of her pupils, but he could also see hope. Maybe even happiness that someone cared.

A worried look appeared on her face. "Help us," she said, "me and Pawpaw?"

Jarod guessed Mary was feeling a bit awkward. Seemed like nobody had ever tried to help her. Nobody had ever cared. Except Pawpaw of course. But that was different. Pawpaw and her needed each other. Sure, some people had felt sorry for them. You probably could see it in their eyes—pity was not what she wanted he was sure. In fact, she probably didn't want anything much, just a happy life and one day she would make sure that she would be in a position to give instead of having to take. He was certain of that.

The little money they sometimes received would, likely, once in a while, buy them a special treat. But this was different. He could sense that she thought *he* was different. This wasn't just about money.

He tried to imagine what she was thinking.

Who is this Jarod? Why is he interested in helping us? Can he also feel that bond? I can see in his eyes that he is different. That he is nice. I don't know what it is, but I can feel it deep inside of me. I can't explain or even understand it, but it is something. A connection, a trust, a link. And it is not like Pawpaw and I don't need the help. Is it possible that this man might be able to help us? Even a little? I don't like the idea of begging, but I know we have no choice, and it is the only way for us to make it.

"Yes," Jarod said, and this time it was him who held Mary under his gaze. He wanted to show her that he meant it when he said he would help them, and he hoped she too could feel the bond he had already felt. "If you and Pawpaw will let me, of course."

Mary turned to Pawpaw, knelt down and took her hand. "Please wait, sir, I tell Pawpaw," she said.

"lâozông Jiâ Luõ Dé xīwàng bângzhù," she said in Chinese.

Pawpaw's toothless smile reappeared wider than ever. She looked up at Jarod and extended her hand.

Jarod took it.

"Xièxiè Jiâ Luõ Dé, nī shigè hâorén," she continued and ignored the blank look on Jarod's face and the frown that

19

followed in an attempt to understand what she was saying.

He had looked at the exchange between Pawpaw and Mary, not understanding what they were saying, but from the smile on Pawpaw's face, he could see she was happy. He took it as a positive sign and smiled back at Pawpaw, nodding reassuringly.

Mary turned back to him, a tear in her eye and a tentative smile of relief. "Okay sir," she said, trying to keep her voice steady. "Pawpaw say you nice man and say thank to you."

Jarod felt his shoulders relax.

He didn't even know his body had been tensed up and a knot held built at the base of his neck until now.

He was relieved. Helping them was the right thing to do. He knew it.

"Great!" he said, almost too loudly. New passer-byes stopped in their strides and added to the increasing already-sizable crowd. He felt like a monkey in a zoo. A ring of heat formed around his neck.

"How do we do this?" he said and scratched his head. Beats of sweat were forming at the base of his hair line. "How is your apartment, Mary? Is it like rundown?"

Mary looked puzzled as if she didn't get what he was asking.

"Oh, I mean, is it old? You know, maybe the paint is old, or maybe things are broken and need repairing?" He sounded as if he were almost begging because he wanted so much to be of help.

Her eyes widened. "Oh, I see!" she said.

Mary let go of Pawpaw's hand and stood up. She looked around and also seemed to notice the new crowd that had formed around their little theatrical performance. It was obvious to Jarrod that she was used to people starring. When you begged in the streets, crowds were something you learned to ignore. You had to learn how to smile whenever someone dropped a coin in the cookie tin.

"Maybe I could, you know, like make it more comfortable

for you and Pawpaw."

Mary smiled. Her eyes once again digging into Jarod. But this time, it wasn't discomfort he felt. He was a sense of well-being and inner joy.

Her thumb and finger pinched her lower lip, and her mouth twisted to one side. "It is not so nice, sir. Paint come out and few things break. And toilet and cooking place together same room, so yes, not so nice."

Jarod wasn't sure he had heard properly. "What did you say? Your toilet and kitchen are in the same room? Is that even legal?"

He wiped the growing beads of sweat from his forehead and took a moment to reflect. "Okay, Mary, would you mind giving me your address? I can come around on the weekend to have a look? Saturday, lunch? My treat."

Mary looked at Pawpaw uncertain. Then her eyes fell back on Jarod like she knew that they had nothing to fear. It was obvious she could see how genuine and concerned Jarod was for them. He was an angel who had fallen from heaven.

"Okay," she said. "Saturday good, sir. Me have no school and Pawpaw maybe no need to be in street. I wait for you home, okay?"

"Sure thing, Mary," he said. He thought for a second. "Can you call me Jarod instead of sir? It feels kind of awkward."

Mary smiled, and it warmed Jarod on the inside to see the happiness in her eyes. He knew it was just a habit that she called older men 'sir'. It was a matter of respect.

"Yes, sir," she said. "I mean Jarod."

Jarod put his hands in his pockets and balanced his weight from one foot to the other. He thought for a few seconds, his mouth to one side.

I guess that's it.

He was just about the leave, but he forgot something. "Guess I'll need an address!" he said. "Do you have a phone number, Mary?"

He noticed Pawpaw still looking at him, her smile frozen into that toothless grin Jarod found so captivating.

The crowd had probably gotten bored by the exchange and was now starting to thin out.

"Yes," Mary said. "My address is 4A ."

"Oh hang on..." Jarod pulled out his cell phone from his pocket and turn it on. "Okay, go ahead, sorry."

Mary reached out for the phone. "Maybe I type address?"

"Yes, sure, I guess it will be easier. And also your phone number, please."

She keyed into the phone with her little fingers typing away. Her tongue was sticking out slightly, and a little frown creased her forehead.

When she finished, she looked up and saw Jarod smiling. She smiled back and handed him back his cell phone.

Jarod looked at the address and phone number.

Sheung Sha Wan.

He knew it was a run-down older district.

He pinched his lips and nodded.

This was the right thing to do. And not just that, he knew this would help him as much as it would Pawpaw and Mary.

"Great." he said and looked at his watch. "I need to go now, Mary."

He took a step forward and extended his hand.

Mary took it, her tiny hand lost in his.

He squeezed it once, let go, and bent down taking Pawpaw's hand in his. It felt like a bird's claw, hardly any flesh on it. He squeezed it and smiled.

Pawpaw looked up at him. A single tear ran down her wrinkled face and settled in one of the deep furrows that crossed her time-worn features.

Jarod let go of her hand.

He took an awkward step forward, one final smile, and walked away.

After a few steps, he looked back.

Both Mary and Pawpaw were staring at him. Both had smiles on their faces.

Jarod felt a tear running down his own face now. He wiped it off absently. He still didn't understand what had just happened. But inside, he knew, he felt something good—he needed it

Then, suddenly without warning, it hit him again at the corner of his right eye.

The shimmer.

CHAPTER 4

"**I** don't know what's wrong with him. I'm really worried," Catalina said rolling the glass in her hand and staring into its amber content.

She looked around.

The room had that nice, cozy darkness. It brought back a memory from when she was a child and used to create a tent out of her bed sheet—her little cocoon, her getaway. Sophie's home always felt like that to her. It was a haven where she could relax and be herself. She could cross her legs and didn't have to behave like a lady.

Her eyes settled on the clock. It was mid afternoon, 3pm on the dot. She felt the whiskey descending and its warmth hitting the pit of her stomach.

A bit early for that but oh well, it might put things into perspective.

Sophie, Catalina's best friend, was sitting across from her. She was sipping a peppermint tea. It seemed more appropriate given the time of day.

Catalina looked up at her. She seemed preoccupied—lost in her own thoughts. Catalina knew her closest friend better than anyone, and she also knew that she loved being single and did not want or need anyone permanent in her life. She enjoyed her independence and, except for the occasional one night stand, she wasn't interested in any of the complications of a relationship. Catalina sometimes wondered if she would feel lonely if she were like her best friend.

Sophie owned a handbag company and bet-ween her yoga and fitness classes and her occasional drinks with friends, there wasn't much time left for romance.

Catalina knew her friend would be too old for love one of these days and would probably come to regret it. But she guessed that was a risk her friend was willing to take—her freedom was way too valuable, and she cherished and guarded it like a dog would his bone.

She was a petite, blonde with blue eyes, and quite a knockout by anyone's standard. Catalina sometimes would feel a pinch of jalousie when looking at her. Her lips were full and her eyes were big and round. You could almost see your reflection in them. It was like looking into a clear blue sea. Her hair was shoulder length, and her skin still retained that golden tan from her last holiday in Côte d'Azur, where she had had the pleasure of an amazing one-night stand with Philippe, an older man she had met during her holidays. Green eyes, fifties, and *very* experienced. Catalina smiled. She knew where her friend's mind was right at that moment.

"Sophie," she said, seeing reality come back to her eyes. "Not thinking of Philippe again by any chance?" Sophie's eyes met hers. "You're such a perv, you know that?" she laughed.

Sophie blushed a little and seemed to regain her composure.

"Ha ha," she laughed and sat back up, her eyes focused now. "You're not my best friend for nothing."

Catalina brought the whiskey to her lips and took a quick sip. "*You!* have a one track mind, Ms Sophie. I wonder how you do it. Don't you ever want to settle down?" She placed her glass back on the glass table and noticed it was already half empty or half full—depending on how you looked at it.

"What for?" Sophie said. She had a pretend-shocked look on her face. " Look at you, are you happy?"

"Ah! So you *have* been listening!" Catalina said. "I'm happy... really. Jarod is great. I'm just, you know, worried about him..."

Sophie took a sip of her tea. "Yes, your were telling me. Is it that shimmer thing again? "

"If only. I almost got used to that, even though it's driving me crazy at times. But it always seems that when we are about to have a good time, that shimmer of his shows up and spoils the moment."

She grabbed the bottle of whiskey, which was within easy reach, and added a couple of fingers to her empty glass—she needed it. She took a long swallow and continued. "But that's not just it, honey, there's something else, and I just can't put my finger on it..."

"Really?" Sophie said. Her eyes narrowed with concern. "Like what?"

"I'm not sure," Catalina said. "He seems more distant lately. Like he has something on his mind. Apart from the shimmer, that is. And when I ask him what's wrong, he says he is okay, that it's just the shimmer. But I don't know, I can feel there is another problem."

Sophie put down her tea and rested her head on her hand. She looked thoughtful.

"Hummm... you don't... think, you know..."

Catalina looked up from her glass, her eyes opened wide. "That he's having an affair?" she just confirmed her own thoughts. It did feel as if he was holding back some secret. She hated the thought of someone else. They hadn't been together for long, but she loved him more than any other man she had been with before. She didn't know why. He wasn't exactly the man of her dreams, but was there such a person? But he was nice, gentle and caring and mostly she knew how much he loved her.

Only now this...

It's possible nothing is going on.

She had tried to convince herself more than once. And maybe it really was only the shimmer. But, she was a woman, and a woman has instincts. And inside, she knew. She knew he was thinking of someone else.

"It's really like his mind is somewhere else," she continued. "This has been happening for the last couple of weeks. And also, he stayed back at work a couple of times this week. Or so he says. And last Sunday, he disappeared for most of the day. He said a friend needed his help to move furniture."

Sophie's lips twisted to one side. She didn't say anything for a minute, then she frowned. "Well, maybe he's telling the truth, Cat. Maybe your imagination is running a bit wild you know? I mean, is it possible that he actually *did* have to stay back and that he *did* have to help someone move house?"

"I don't know, honey. Maybe you're right. I really hope you are…"

Catalina drank the last of her whiskey and grimaced at the sudden heat she felt cascading down her wind-pipe. She winced and smacked her lips. "We haven't really been together for that long but I think I really like him."

Sophie's eyes narrowed and a side-way smirk settled upon her face. "Oh… love is it?"

"Ha ha," Catalina laughed, waving off the romantic thought and feeling the heat rushing to her face. "Well, I wouldn't go that far! But… there is definitely something…" She recomposed herself. "Well, anyway. Unlike you Ms Flirty-pants, I do like the idea of having one man on my mind and maybe, who knows... settling down doesn't sound so bad."

"No thanks!" Sophie said and crossed her arms. "Not for this black duck! I like my life the way it is, and there's no way I'll ever want to settle down."

Catalina didn't react, she just sat there, staring into nothingness.

Sophie frowned. "Soooo... you really think so? You really think that there is more? Or maybe it's really just your imagination. I mean, you guys make such a great couple. I would hate to see it end. Well, especially since you seem so happy with him..."

Catalina shook her head, not wanting to believe that this was really happening—not wanting to admit it.

"Yes," she finally said. "I am sure, and that's also the problem. I'm happy. For once, I have found the right guy and I just don't know what to do..." She looked down at her glass of whiskey. It was empty. She was feeling a little light-headed, but maybe she needed one more finger to put things into perspective. Her eyes fell back on her friend. "Can I have another one? I think I need it..."

"Sure," Sophie said. "Although it is a bit early to be downing three. But then hey... you only live once right?"

Sophie got up and poured another shot into Catalina's glass. "There you go babe," she said. "Don't drink it all at once, okay? Anyway, it'll make you feel better."

"Thanks, honey," Catalina said and took a tiny sip. "I'm glad I have you to talk to. What would I do without you?"

"Hey... what are friends for?" Sophie said, taking Catalina's hand and squeezing it lightly, her lips curling up into a comforting smile.

CHAPTER 5

Jarod was standing at the building's entrance. He could barely see the dark interior with the narrows stairs. In was the middle of the day and the sun was shining, but it was not able to penetrate the gloomy, dark hallway.

Mary had said Flat 4A. He looked up and counted four levels. He wasn't sure which one was Pawpaw's and Mary's window, but it didn't really matter—there were all covered in grime and the facade surrounding them was in serious need of repair.

Like spider webs covering the outside wall, antenna wires dangled from the rooftop—each wire descending to reach a gap in a window, dutifully giving its owner an emission of televised happiness in an otherwise dark and damp existence.

Jarod slowly crept in. With each steps, he felt like he was being swallowed up by the engulfing darkness.

The stairs were narrow and filthy. Between the second and third floor, he found himself looking at—he wasn't sure what... shit? Human shit? Dog shit? When the emitted gases finally reached his nostrils, he could feel his eyes watering and the bile rising at the back of his throat made him retch a couple of times. He felt his knees buckle and his hand had to find the nearest greasy wall so as not to land on the defecation. His sense of smell definitely confirmed that it was shit, and by the foul yet familiar scent—human shit. He managed to swallow back down the bitter bile, pinched his nose between his thumb and index and took a giant step to get across the mystery feces, hoping that he wouldn't slip on the yellow puddle that was surrounding it like a yellow sea encircling a molten crap island.

How could anyone live in this place? Wasn't it bad enough to have to go up those dark stairs everyday, only to find out that some asshole had decided to take a dump in the middle of the third floor landing?

Jarod felt disgusted. The thought of his comfortable, clean home with its modern interior made him feel guilty, knowing that Pawpaw and Mary had to walk up these very same stairs everyday and go through an obstacle course of urine and shit just to make it home.

Finally, he reached the fourth floor, and it wasn't nearly soon enough.

There was a main gate made of green, rusted iron and beyond that, a decaying wall. He guessed it would have been green once but now he wasn't sure as most of the paint had long ago vanished to powder.

A small corridor veered left and Jarod was only able to see a few feet beyond the locked gate before the corridor made a right turn.

There was no bell.

Jarod started knocking on the thick iron gate, and only a dull sound met his ears, as if the stench of dampness and shit were absorbing everything around them.

There was no way that Mary would hear that.

He felt frustrated, being stuck in this smelly entombment whilst pounding the gate with his fist, to the point where he knew a bruise would eventually appear.

The sound that resonated was a bit louder this time, but he doubted Mary would have been able to hear it, especially since he didn't know how far the little corridor wound its way around to her sub-divided apartment.

He gave up and pulled out his cell phone. He dialed Mary's number.

He waited a few rings and was about to give up to when he heard a click as the connection was made.

"Waiii?" answered a small, nasal, uncertain voice.

Jarod didn't recognize the voice and wasn't sure if it was Mary on the other end.

"Err," he hesitated. "Hello? This is Jarod. Is this Mary?"

The small voice was silent for a moment and then "Waiiii? Waiii? Who?"

This time Jarod recognized her voice.

"Jarod. Remember me?" he queried. "I met you and Pawpaw in the street."

Finally Jarod heard recognition in her small voice. "Oh Jarod! Yes, me remember! Where you?"

"I'm inside your building. Well, on the fourth floor actually, but there is no doorbell at the front gate. I've tried to knock but I guess you couldn't hear me."

"Oh! Sorry," Mary said, "you wait Jarod, me coming. You stay, okay?"

"Okay, Mary. I'll wait right here for you." He hoped he wouldn't have to wait too long and wondered how much more of the putrid smell his senses would be able to absorb without going into verbal extraction mode— adding a new smell to the concoction.

He put his cell phone back into his back pocket and waited. A minute in this place was more painful than a minute in a plank position.

He heard a door being pushed hard with a bang from around the narrow corridor. Footsteps were coming towards him and suddenly, there was Mary.

She smiled from ear to ear. It warmed Jarod's heart. He wasn't sure how it would go and whether Mary would remember him. After all, how many people passed them in the street? But she did, and it showed.

"Hello Jarod," she said in her tiny voice. "This is first time someone come here. Oh and sorry, me forget tell you no bell."

31

He heard the latch, and Mary put her full forty-eight pounds into it and pushed the iron gate with a grunt. Finally, the gate opened, and Jarod was able to escape the soiled and putrid stairway.

He followed her down the narrow passage. The light green paint that once had been was peeling, and the damp smell filled his lungs. The narrow, dark hallway was barely wide enough for his not-so-broad shoulders and he could see that it ended just a few feet down. There were three doors. One facing him and two flanking it.

The three entrances to the sub-divided lodgings were totally mismatched and were all but flimsy rotted planks of woods. Probably barely enough to resist a cat brushing against them—great security, Jarod thought.

Mary's and Pawpaw's flat was the one on the right. The door was slightly ajar but Mary still had to get her frail shoulder into it to push it open. It gave way and slammed into whatever was blocking it from the inside.

"Well, guess first order of business will be that door. A little WD40 should do the trick."

Mary stepped in.

Jarod followed.

As he entered, he almost ran into her back. He looked up and noticed she couldn't really have gone any further, even if she had wanted to—the front wall facing her was a mere five feet away.

He looked around while Mary squeezed around him to shut the door. The room was tiny. Really tiny. It didn't take much for him to take it all in.

He was standing three feet from the entrance, and he would only have had to extend his hand to touch the wall facing him.

Directly to his left was a small bedroom. It looked to be around nine-by-six feet, and he could see a double bed hand-made from planks. It was elevated four feet high so as to accommodate a double set of wooden doors that were simply cut into the six-by-four side board. The bed took up most of the space in the room and upon it sat and assortment of covers, blankets and clothes.

"Mmmmm, at least they have enough layers to keep warm."

Next to the bed was a tiny desk overloaded with books, and Jarod wondered how Mary was able to do her homework. The walking space was barely enough to take two steps before reaching the desk.

The lounge-dining area was astoundingly smaller than the bedroom. It was six-by-six, and facing Jarod were two small cane lounge chairs that had seen better days, and a minuscule about-to-burst wardrobe.

He turned his head, and to his right he saw behind the door a small fridge that barely reached his waist and a television sitting upon it. The television was on but the picture that was trying to appear made a snow storm in New York look mild in comparison.

Jarod took a single step to the right and saw the kitchen/bathroom/toilet combination Mary had told him about.

Mary looked at him and let him take it all in. The room was around two feet wide, and he assumed six feet long as it ran along the west lounge room wall.

He peered discreetly inside and saw a toilet at one end with a shower head attached to a filthy, grayish, cracked tiled wall. He had to look twice and his jaw dropped.

The *kitchen* was basically a sink, obviously used to wash you hands after dropping your load…and to wash the dishes. Next to the sink was a mini gas stove, the kind you'd bring camping with you, with a small assortment of various cooking utensils sitting in a plastic box. A rice cooker sat in the corner and a twisted coat hanger was used above the stove to hold a frying pan.

The bathroom-kitchen had a layer of grime that seemed to be part of the decor. It resembled a mixture of ejaculated oil from the frying pan, and god-knows what else.

Jarod shuddered at the thought of having to come into contact with that wall should the need to use the toilet arise. Something that would almost seem inevitable given the constraints of the impossibly confined area.

He took a whiff but to his surprise, the room did not have the unpleasant smell that would be expected of its greasy entourage. The smell resembled slightly of a damp cloth that had been sitting around for too long. But apart from that, it was bearable. Well, unless someone had to use the shit-house whilst Pawpaw was cooking.

He had another shudder.

After a minute of taking in the scenery, Mary's little voice snapped him out of his trance. "Sit down please." She pointed to one of the cane chairs.

Pawpaw was not home, and that wasn't hard to figure out vis-à-vis the size of the place. Jarod thought maybe she was in the streets, looking as miserable as she could in order to make passersby feel sorry for her and dig deep into their pockets for loose change that would find their way into her tin box.

Jarod finally sat. The cane lounge chair was actually pretty comfortable.

"You like drink?" Mary asked cheerfully.

"Sure," Jarod replied and tried to dispel the shock look that must have seemed obvious on his face. "What do you have?"

"Have water and tea."

"Water it is then."

Mary stepped into the *kitchen*.

Jarod saw Mary take a glass from the plastic box and pour water from a once-transparent plastic carafe. Its yellowness made Jarod wonder what color the water was, but he felt a sense of relief when it emerged clear. He hoped the water had been boiled as the thought of getting poisoned from a cup of water didn't seem too appealing.

He grabbed the glass handed out to him and peered discretely into it whilst Mary was busy sitting herself down on the adjacent seat. There were no floaters inside, so he took that as a good sign.

"So," he said, clearing his throat and feeling a bit awkward sitting in this tiny room with the young girl. "This is home then, hey?"

"Yes," Mary said and looked uneasy herself. "This is home for me and Pawpaw."

Jarod took a tentative sip of the water. It was fresh and actually tasted nice. His parched throat needed it.

"Well, it's not exactly what I had expected. I mean it's... *cozy*, but it's pretty old."

Mary looked down at her hands as if seeing them for the first time. She seemed a bit embarrassed. "Yes, me and Pawpaw live here for one year already. Sometime is okay, sometime is not. Sometime is too hot and sometime is too cold. More for Pawpaw."

Jarod looked around. The small room seemed to be lacking any kind of air conditioning or heater.

"Your mean you don't have any fan or heater?" he asked.

"No. Pawpaw think no need, and she say also cost many money for heater and fan."

"I see..." He wondered how cold it could get in here during winter. It's not as if Hong Kong got extremely cold at around fifty degrees in winter, but still, he could imagine Mary and Pawpaw spending their days cocooned inside the covers of the elevated bed, trying in vain to stay warm. So many people took things for granted, and yet so many more had it so bad. Jarod never imagined people could live like this in Hong Kong. He had seen poor people going around, and he could only imagine what it would be like, but actually being here and seeing it with his own eyes was a shockingly different thing.

He said, "What do you normally do on weekends while Pawpaw is out?"

Mary looked up at him. "Sometime me go out and do food shopping for me and Pawpaw. There is market not far. But most time me stay home and watch TV and do homework."

Jarod took another sip of his water. "You don't have any friends?"

She nodded. "I have one friend. His name is Man Yin. He is good friend but he busy sometime on weekend. He study hard and he has class."

"Classes?"

"Yes, they extra class. Have to pay money."

"Oh I see!" Jarod said when he realized what Mary meant.

"Yes," Mary said and looked a bit confused. "Tutor for extra curr.....lum..."

"Curriculum," Jarod said. "Don't worry, I know it's a difficult word. Actually, I was wondering..."

Suddenly, Jarod felt a jab in his right eye. The pain was unbearable, as if someone was pushing from inside his head. His eye felt as it was going to pop right out. He closed it tightly and tried to hold it in so that the pain would go away, but this only seemed to make it worse.

The shimmer.

Not now, please, not the fucking shimmer.

Even with his eyes shut, Jarod saw it. Right there, right at the corner, as if it had been waiting for the right moment— mocking him.

Then, he *saw* it. A movement. Just like a shadow going past. But there was no one! Just Mary and him…and his eyes were closed!

Mary saw Jarod's face twisted in a contortion of pain—a thick purple vein had appeared on his forehead, his skin red from the blood rushing into it. She panicked, and as she got up to make a move towards Jarod, he fell to the ground holding his head.

"Jarod! Jarod!" she cried, "You okay? What wrong?"

"My god! My head! My eye! What's happening to me!" He was in agony.

The piercing pain was driving deep into his eyeball. It felt as if a nail was being hammered into his skull and the eyeball was the entry point. He imagined his eye bursting out of its socket and landing in the toilet's grimy tiled floor. Laying in shit, staring back at him.

Mary could see her friend on the floor in a fetal position. His hands were holding his head and his finger tips were white from the pressure he was applying to his forehead.

Jarod's mouth was opened in an agonizing grimace but no sound was escaping—his body was shaking with uncontrolled spasms.

Mary stumbled to her friend and tried in vain to lift him up into a seating position but he was way too heavy. She grunted and tried again by putting her skeletal arms under his armpits and pulling as hard as she could.

She gave up and sat on the ground with her a skinny legs sticking straight out and delicately put Jarod's head on her lap. She looked down and saw the beads of sweat running down his face. The spasms contorting his body were making his head loll from side to side and made it hard for Mary to hold onto.

It took all her efforts just to stop his head from hitting the concrete floor.

Another shadow—human? Like someone going past him while he was walking in a street. It was just a shadow, but it was so real! He knew he wasn't dreaming, the shadow was really there.

The pain subsided a little and Mary saw his face relax.

And then, he sank.

Mary felt the convulsions subside, then stop altogether.

37

Jarod's body was limp, like a rag doll. His head resting on Mary's lap rolled to the left. He was looking up at the ceiling. The right eye was half opened and through the small gap, Mary could see the white—only the white, as if Jarod's eyeball had rolled up inside his head.

Mary tried not to panic. She knew she needed to call someone but her was phone sitting on the coffee table. She tried to reach it. Almost—her fingers touched it. She managed to slowly slide it towards her on the glass top. She didn't want to let go of Jarod's head. She didn't want to do that, he needed her—almost there.

Her cell dropped on the concrete floor.

She heard the screen smash and saw bits of glass spread around the phone that was now sitting on its face. She picked it up, careful not to cut her herself. The phone was staring back at her blankly. Her fingers opened and she saw her cell land on the floor next too her.

After a minute, she shook her head. She had to think fast.

She searched Jarod's pockets and found his cell phone. She flicked it open and pressed the call key—a screen appeared: PASSWORD.

An underscore line and a blinking cursor were waiting for her to enter the password she didn't know.

She looked at Jarod and dropped the phone.

A hot involuntarily tear ran down her innocent, discouraged face. She took Jarod's face in her small hands and cradled it like a baby.

She waited.

Then, she dozed off—like a mother holding her infant.

****

He could hear the traffic coming from below. His body felt cold and he was lying on something hard. His head, however, was resting on something soft and warm. It felt good to have his eyes closed. He tried to remember.

How come his bed was feeling so hard? He tried to open his eyes. It felt as if they had been sealed shut. There was a damp smell. He could almost taste it.

Slowly, as if he were pushing a heavy door, his eyelids opened and let a sliver of light through his eyelashes. He could now discern a face right above his.

A young face.

His eyes fluttered.

He was feeling lost.

The face was slim and the cheekbones accentuated. There was spittle at the corner of the overturned mouth. Her eyes were closed, and Jarod could see the smear of a single, dried-up tear that had made its way down the child's face. He recognized her now...

Mary.

And it all came back to him.

The searing pain in his right eye, enough for him to have wanted to tear his eyeball out.

The shimmer.

And...the shadow.

Yes, there had definitely been a shadow, right there, just behind the pain.

He closed his eyes and tried to remember.

It was as if he had been standing behind a dirty window on a dark night. A shadowy figure had moved passed his field of vision. It had been hazy, but he was sure it had been human in shape. He was sure he had not been asleep. How could he have been anyway with the pain shooting into his right eye?

He knew he couldn't have imagined the whole scenario. Why was he lying on a cold, hard floor with his head on Mary's lap?

He imagined he must have been out for quite a while for Mary to have fallen asleep.

Slowly he opened his eyes fully.

He wanted to get up.

He needed to get up.

But he felt heavy.

And tired.

The pain had sucked all the energy from him. He felt like an empty sack, discarded after having been emptied out.

"Mary," he whispered hoarsely. He could hardly hear his own voice. "Mary, can you hear me?"

He tried to lift his hand to Mary's face. He couldn't—it weighted like lead. With a colossal effort, he focused his mind on his right arm and managed to move it one inch.

Then two.

Like a fish swimming through a thick mud puddle, his hand ultimately found its way to Mary's face. His fingers barely touched her right cheek, like a butterfly landing softly.

"Mary," he whispered, this time a little louder. "Mary, wake up. I'm okay now, Mary. Wake up."

Mary's head wobbled to the right as if her pencil neck was having difficulty supporting it. It ended up now resting on Jarod's extended hand. Slowly, her eyes opened. One lid at a time, as if coming out of a trance. She seemed dazed as if she didn't know where she was. Her eyes found Jarod's.

"It's okay, Mary," he said, trying to sound convincing but knowing the probably sounded dead. "It's me. I think...my head. I fell."

Mary finally seemed to be coming back to her senses. He saw recognition in her eyes. The vagueness had vanished from them and her pupils dilated in acknowledgment.

Jarod didn't know how long she had been sitting there, against the wall, with his head on her lap.

It must have been a long time.

"Jarod," she mumbled. "You okay? You fell on floor and hold head and scream. And... and me don't know what to do." A sob escaped her lips. "Me want call police and broke phone and…and can't use you phone."

Jarod saw a tear forming on her lower eyelid. It grew and then ran down to eventually meet her lip. He wiped the tear with his thumb.

"Oh Mary.... it's okay. There is no need to call the police." He tried to smile reassuringly, not really sure how it came out. "I'm okay."

He tried to get his head up and felt the room spin. He rested back on Mary's lap.

"It's the shimmer," he whispered, more to himself than to Mary. "It seems to be getting worse…"

"Shimmer? What is shimmer? Me don't understand shimmer."

"It's hard to explain. It's like a light. No, more like a wave. And I can see it just at the corner of my eye. It seems to be getting worse and worse. And just now, I don't know… it felt as if my head was going to explode." Jarod closed his eyes and remembered the agonizing pain. "It was unbearable Mary…" He looked up at her. Her eyes were big and moist. He could see his face in them. "I'm so sorry that I scared you," he said.

"No, please Jarod," Mary begged. "No need for sorry. Is okay! Me is sorry no call doctor. Me don't know what to do."

"There is nothing a doctor *can* do," he said. "I have been to the doctor already and he thinks it's all in my mind. I think they don't have a clue what's going on to be honest."

Jarod began to feel a bit stupid lying on Mary's lap. He tried lifting his head again but the world around him was still spinning. He let it drop back on her lap.

"Sorry Mary," he apologized once again. "Is my head heavy? It's still spinning a bit."

"No, is okay," Mary said. She gently laid her tiny hand on Jarod's head.

It felt warm and Jarod, finding comfort in her caring response, closed his eyes.

After a few seconds, he opened them again. He was afraid he might doze off. He said, "Listen, why don't you help me up and I'll try to get back on the seat?"

Mary took Jarod's head his her hands and tried with all her might to pull him up to a sitting position.

Slowly, she managed to lift him up from the floor and sit him against the wall with his legs splayed out in front of him.

Jarod looked like a marionette that had been discarded in a corner. His limbs felt like a dead weight, and his head lolled to one side.

He looked around.

Damn this room is small! How can they live in this place? Maybe they are used to it by now. It's not like they have much choice, anyway.

He slowly tried to get into a crouching position by using the wall to push against. Eventually he managed to slide himself up inch-by-inch. Breathing hard from the effort, he laid against the wall and made sure his head stopped swimming before attempting to make the seemingly impossible journey to the cane chair that sat a mere two feet away.

He focused like an athlete attempting to smash the long-jump world record. His eyes never left the chair as his mind visualized the steps to make the impossible possible.

He wobbled like he had too much to drink.

Mary stepped under him, tip-toeing to bear his weight and setting her shoulder in the crook of his arm-pit.

Jarod let some of his weight settle on Mary's small frame but worried she might collapse and send them both crashing in a tangle of limbs.

But she was stronger than she looked. Her skinny legs managed to hold him up and after a few small, unsteady steps, she had Jarod slumped into the nearest cane chair.

"I get you glass of water," she said, her chest heaving up and down from the effort.

Jarod was grateful and smiled at her. What would he have done without her?

She turned around. and Jarod could see her sweaty tee-shirt stuck against her bony back, her ribs making her brown shirt look like sand dunes in a desert.

She can't be more than fifty pounds.

While Mary was getting the water, Jarod settled back in his seat.

I wonder what that was.

The image he saw seemed so real. It was as if he had been behind a dirty glass window looking out. And then, it seemed as if someone had just walked past the window. It definitely hadn't felt like a dream—it had felt so real.

"Here you go," Mary said and made Jarod jump. She handed him the glass of water and settled herself into the only other chair in the room.

This time, Jarod didn't look into the glass to see if the water looked potable. He gulped it down and let it parch the desert that had settled in his throat.

When done he handed the empty glass back to Mary.

"Could I have another one please," he asked. "I'm as dry as a bone."

"Dry as what?" Mary asked and looked confused.

"Dry as... never-mind. Could I just have another glass please?" he smiled.

He could hear the water being poured from the yellowish jug and to his right, the sound of cars reaching him from four floors below.

What is happening to me? This is crazy—why me?

Everything around him seemed so normal. Why couldn't things be normal for him? What had he done to deserve this? Even the damn doctor didn't have a clue as to what was wrong with him. And they called themselves doctors? They probably wouldn't be able to diagnose a hemorrhoid sticking out of their own ass. Most of them probably took a half-ass guess most of the time, and most of us were too dumb to trust our bodies to them.

Well not this black duck If they can't find out what's wrong with me, then I'm just gonna have to figure it out by myself.

A shadow fell upon Jarod. Lost in his own thoughts, he momentarily forgot where he was. His eyes focused and there was Mary with a glass of water in her hand.

But something was wrong.

She was just standing there.

Her hand was shaking and water was spilling from the edge of the glass, the droplets forming a paddle on the concrete floor.

Her eyes were fixed. Her lower lip trembled slightly, and Jarod saw a tear forming at the corner of her eye.

"Mary?" he whispered, a bead of sweat on his brow. "What's wrong Mary? Are you okay?"

"My... my eye."Her left hand rose up to her eye, her right hand still holding the glass.

Jarod saw her fingers starting to loosen and the glass sliding down between them. He managed to catch it in time and set it on the glass top table.

"Mary, what's wrong with your eye?" He felt the heat around his collar.

"I...I don't know." Her voice was shaky. The tear found its way down her cheek and joined the water puddle that had formed from the spilled glass. "It's like a light and—it's moving."

"Moving?" He didn't like what he was hearing. "What do you mean moving? You mean like a shimmer? Is that what you see Mary? Do you see it? Do you see the shimmer?"

The tone in Jarod's voice had risen. There was excitement and fear at the same time. Could this be possible? How could it be possible? Not Mary. Please not her. What's going on? Had he somehow passed it on to her? Could it be contagious? How could a fucked up eye be contagious?

His mind raced with possibilities.

He had hardly touched her.

44

And even if he did, how could anything contagious be passed on so quickly? He wasn't a doctor but he knew it just didn't make any sense.

Mary's arms suddenly dropped, and she stared into emptiness like a cordless marionette.

Jarod stood up and held her by the shoulders, making sure she wasn't going to sag and crumble to the ground like he did. It didn't take much effort to hold her up.

"Mary, tell me what your see. Tell me now before it goes away. Do you see a man, Mary? Do you? Like…like someone going passed maybe?"

Mary's eyes closed and her right hand flew to her face in what seemed to Jarod like his own attempt at stopping the shimmer.

She must be seeing it.

Jarod knew it was pointless.

It would still be there, even with her eyes closed.

It couldn't be stopped anymore than a car without breaks heading for a tree.

Suddenly, her hand dropped and her face was back to normal.

Just like that.

Just like *it* had never been there in the first place.

She opened her eyes.

Jarod's face was only a few inches from hers.

He saw the concern in her eyes. He felt as if she was trying to look into his soul. To search for something—to search for an answer.

He grabbed her, his fingers unwillingly digging into her shoulders.

He needed to know what she had seen.

Jarod sensed Mary tried to get away and he tightened his grip. He peered deeply into her eyes. His eyes shifted to her right eye. He wanted to see something—anything.

But there was nothing to see.

Mary's eyes looked totally normal, except for the now dried up tear that had smeared a path down her face.

Not a trace of the shimmer remained.

"You hurting me!" she cried-out, eyes wide with fear.

Jarod reluctantly let go.

"Sorry, Mary, sorry, I didn't mean to. I'm sorry…"

Mary took a step back. She looked like a frightened puppy. She was shaking.

"Please Mary, I'm sorry," he begged. "I didn't mean to scare you. I was scared myself. It's me Mary… Jarod."

Jarod raised his hands in surrender. They were shaking. He could see the mistrust and fear in Mary's young face. He needed her to trust him. He needed her, because he was sure she had also seen *it*.

"Mary," he said, "I promise I won't hurt you. I didn't mean to grab your shoulder so hard. I was worried. I was worried you were going to pass out like I did…"

He saw her tense body relax ever so slightly.

She lifted her hand and dropped it into his own open one. He squeezed it and smiled reassuringly.

The tension seemed to have slowly dissipated from her body.

He felt her trust coming back—the recognition.

Hesitantly she smiled just to let him know she was okay.

Jarod felt an enormous sense of relief.

"Sit down Mary," he said and let go of her hand. "Tell me what you saw."

She eased herself into the adjacent chair, her body sagging. "Is not first time I see wave."

A rattling of keys.

Mary and Jarod eyes turned toward the front door at the same time.

A click and then the door was pushed opened.

Pawpaw's prune face appeared and her gaped smile reminded Jarod of tomb stones scattered across a graveyard.

Her genuine happiness at seeing him created even more wrinkles than he would have thought possible.

"Hello," she said and stepped inside the apartment. She closed the door behind her and stood there looking back at the two white figures staring blankly back at her.

"Oh, hello," Jarod said as he finally came out of his trance. "I was just leaving actually…"

Bad timing. I will need to talk to Mary later.

He rushed out of the apartment without saying goodbye.

He descended the dark, damp stairway. His mind tried to make sense of the events that had just taken place.

What's going on. It's not just me now, it's also Mary.

It seemed impossible.

How could both of them see the shimmer? Was it possible that he had passed it on to her? Could the shimmer be contagious?

He reached the bottom of the stairway and was glad to leave the smelly confines and feel the sun on his upturned face. It was good to be out of there.

He turned right and he took the direction of the subway. He was walking in a daze, his footsteps leading him automatically in the right direction. He still wasn't sure what had happened, if it even had happened at all.

The shimmer.

Him passing out.

Waking up in Mary's arms—on the floor.

And then Mary.

She had seen it too. He was sure if it.

Was that the connection he had felt the first time he had met her? It must have been. He had known when they first met that there was something different about her. Could it be that both of them were incomprehensibly, somehow connected together by the shimmer? Was it possible that there was a link? Like some kind of magnetic field that they both could see? And feel?

47

Mary was the first person he had met who could also see it. She was probably the only person, so far, who didn't think he was crazy. Could there be others?

He had reached the station.

He stopped halfway down the stairs.

He wasn't crazy after all! Mary was the proof. She was the undeniable confirmation that he hadn't lost his mind.

Now what? Maybe they could try to find out, together what the hell was going on?

His feet continued their descent into the depth of the underground tube.

One step after another, taking him aimlessly.

A lost soul.

CHAPTER 6

Catalina leaned forward. "So you actually expect me to believe that?" She looked pissed. "Not only did you spend the afternoon with a kid and her grandma, supposedly out of compassion, but, as convenient as it may seem, your battery was flat, so you weren't able to call me."

Jarod's armpits moistened, as if he were actually guilty. His body sank slowly into the couch. "Babe, I swear it's the truth! Now come on, believe me! Why would I lie to you?" His tone was defensive.

He knew she didn't believe him, and unfortunately for him looking nervous didn't help. She knew him and she knew him well. She *knew* when he was lying, even when he wasn't—guilty before proven innocent.

"Well," she said sarcastically, "how fortunate that your cell phone happened to run out of battery just when *you* happened to be missing all afternoon."

"You have to believe me!" His hands began to feel moist. Damn, why was she making him feel so nervous? Was it because the truth always seems so far-fetched? Like a bullshit made-up story? Maybe a lie would have been better than the truth that actually sounded like bullshit.

49

"And why should I?" she said. "You know, and I know, and we both know that *that* is the worst excuse you could come up with. At least you could have given me the recognition of being a little bit smarter than you and could have thought of an excuse I might actually believe. *This*, in itself, is an insult!"

She stood up.

Jarod remained on his chair, a lamb at the slaughter.

Her eyes pierced through him. If looks could kill, he would have been six feet under right there and then.

He swallowed hard. "Listen to me, will you?" he said in a pathetic voice he hated the sound off—that stupid voice that made you sound guilty no matter what.

She took a step closer. "No! You listen to me, *asshole!*" She was now yelling, her face mere inches from his. "You know exactly what you're doing! So stop the bullshit ,okay? I'm not some cheap little darling whore you can just lie to and get away with it!"

He could feel heat emanating from both his and her body —the heat of hell that was about to break loose.

She said, "You wanna double-time me and think you can get away with it? Well, you've got another thing coming. I'm not going to put up with this shit. Don't you think I know what's going on?" She was enraged.

Jarod sank into his seat and felt like a kid being scolded by his mother. He swore he could see smoke emerging from her flared nostrils.

"What's her fucking name?" she went on.

"What?" he choked. "Is that what you think?"

"It's not what I think, I know!"

He tried to reassure her, reaching out for her hand. "Babe, I love you. What are you saying? There's not way I would do such a thing and jeopardize what we have."

"Oh, yes, you would! In fact, any guy would. Because you guys are all the same. All you do is think with your cock, and as soon as an opportunity presents itself, you don't think twice

50

and just hope you won't get caught. Well, this time, though, I got news for you. Not only you did you get caught, but I won't let you get away with it."

Drops of nervous perspiration formed high up on his forehead. This was not looking good. Why couldn't she believe him?

"I swear I'm telling you the truth, okay?" he said in an attempt to make her see some sense. "What do you want me to do? Lie to you to make you feel better? You are right, I could have had a better excuse if I *had* wanted to lie to you. But the reason I didn't lie is because I'm telling you the truth!"

Catalina sat back down. Her eyes narrowed and her features softened. "Okay," she said, her tone dropping a pitch. "Then prove it."

"How?" Jarod queered hopeful. "Anything at all babe."

"Give me that kid's number so I can call her."

"Err, that's not possible," Jarod said remembering how Mary had told him she had broken her cell. "She…"

"What? She doesn't have a phone now?"

"No! No, she broke it when she was…" Jarod knew this sounded like more bullshit. "You don't understand, babe…"

"When she was what? Fucking you?" she said, surprisingly calm. "Oh yes, I understand perfectly well…" This wasn't a good sign. Maybe it was better when she was angry. "I understand that I wasn't good enough for you, and you were not able to keep your dick in your pants. I also understand that I don't have to put up with this shit, and that there are plenty of guys out there that would treasure me. And *me* only."

"Are you breaking up with me? Babe? Come on…"

First the shimmer, and now *this*? She was the only thing that kept him going.

"No! There is *no way* I'll put up with your cheating!" she was now screaming.

Jarod was getting desperate. "Babe! I'll prove it to you! Let's go there right now, and you can meet Mary. Then you'll know I'm telling you the truth, okay?"

"Oh, yeah?" she said cynically. "It's way too easy for you two to have made up some sort of story to pretend you were over there. Maybe you bought that kid a lunch or whatever, and she'll say whatever you want."

His shirt was sticking to his back, the damp smell of fear and loss emanating from every pore filled his nostrils. "What? Are you serious This is ridiculous! I am willing to take you there and prove to you. I am telling the truth, and you don't trust me? What am I supposed to do?"

He stopped there—he was lost for words. How could this be happening? She really didn't believe him! He loved her, and she was the best thing that had ever happened to him. Why didn't she trust him? Why couldn't she see how much he cared for her? He knew most guys did screw around, but he wasn't most guys. He had always been a faithful man. So why would he start cheating now? Couldn't she see that?

"I'm begging you, babe." He gave one last attempt. "I'm begging you to trust me on this. I'm not doing anything wrong. I swear."

"Oh! You swear now, do you?" she said mockingly. "Suddenly you have a conscience and became a good boy? Your swearing doesn't mean *shit* to me. For all I know, you don't even go to church, so swearing isn't going to make me believe anything you say."

Jarod's shoulder slumped. "Okay, I give up." He knew there was no way he could make her believe him. She had made up her mind, and no matter what he said, she wasn't going to change it. "It's obvious you don't trust me and believe I am cheating on you. Go ahead and believe what you want. I have done nothing wrong and my conscience is clear."

Catalina sat back. She also seemed to have finally given up the will to argue. Her face showed sadness and betrayal. He looked at the face he loved so much. She looked so hurt and defeated. It made him feel guilty, but guilty for what? He hadn't done anything wrong, and the thought of cheating on her had never even occurred to him.

Sure, there had been some instances when others girls did eyeball him at the bar or even in the office. And sure, any guys would have been tempted. But, Jarod knew that he had something special here, and he could really see a future with Catalina. For the first time in his pathetic life, he actually believed that he had actually found what love was.

And now—now he was about to lose her. All because she didn't trust him. How ironic. How stupid it all was. He was about too lose everything he cared about.

He rose from his seat and knelt in front of her. It broke his heart to see her like that. Her eyes were staring straight ahead, seeing nothing. A lone tear fell and landed on her lap, forming a tiny pool on her leg. And then a stream, flowing slowly down her white inner thigh—like a gentle river current weeping on an early spring day.

The feeling of helplessness rose in him like something stuck in his throat, and no matter how hard he swallowed, it just wouldn't go down. He was going to lose her. He felt it deep inside. Between the damn shimmer and now this, there didn't seem to be any hope left in this relationship. What had he done to deserve this?

If it hadn't been for this damn shimmer, he wouldn't have gone to see Mary. Well, that really didn't have anything do to with it, did it? Or maybe, it did. He wouldn't have felt the connection, right there and then, in the street, when he had first seen her.

Did the shimmer have anything do to with them meeting up or was it just a coincidence?

Nothing made sense anymore.

And now this.

Catalina.

The one girl he really loved.

And she didn't trust him.

Catalina looked up. "It's a shame, Jarod, I really did love you." Her voice was shaking. She was sobbing.

"Did?" he took her hand in his. "Babe, what are you saying?"

She pulled it away.

She clenched her teeth, her eyes never leaving his, her face hardened. "What I'm saying is that whatever you did, you are not going to do again—not to me anyway."

Jarod knew all was lost. He knew his words would not change anything. But he had to try. "Listen, if I did do something wrong, I would be the first one to admit it. But, babe, I didn't. Please, you have to trust me."

"I don't." She straightened up and seemed in control again. He saw the determination in her eyes, and it scared him. "I know what men are like, and I don't believe you. We had a good thing going. But I guess it wasn't good enough for you."

This time, another tear pooled and fell to the ground.

But the tear was not Catalina's.

CHAPTER 7

"**W**hat *is* wrong with you, Jarod?"

He hated it when his boss Margaret hovered over him like a giant panda. Damn, not a panda—a panda was way to cute to be compared to this great lump of shit. God he hated her.

"What do you mean, what's wrong?" Jarod said, feeling more pissed by the minute.

"Jarod. This is the third project we've had to delay due to your incompetence." She said it loud enough to make sure the whole damn floor could hear her. "This is not good enough! The users have been screaming because they were supposed to have this new bonus point system initiated during the last quarter, and now they are not even going to get it in this quarter, just because Mr. Johnson can't get his act together and do his job on time."

Jarod could now feel it without seeing it. All eyes were on him. Why did that bitch always have to make such a show of power in front of everybody? Just because she was single, and no one would be caught dead shagging the fat slag, didn't mean she had to take out her frustration out on him.

He straightened up on his chair and tried to look more confident than he felt. He could already feel the stain building up under his right armpit. He didn't know why but it was already the right armpit that copped it when he was nervous—one of the reasons he never wore a dark shirt.

"Wait a minute," he said, "this project was doomed to start with. I had originally estimated it to seven-hundred man days, and *you* chopped it down to five-hundred. Also, I needed six resources, and you only gave me four." That's it baby, you lay it out to the bitch.

She opened her mouth to reply, but he didn't let her and made sure that his voice was as loud as hers. "Then! When shit hits the fan, you come to me and start complaining!"

He saw her eyes widen with disbelief and her lower lip tremble—oh, the satisfaction. Suck on that…bitch!

"How dare you speak to me like that, Mr. Johnson?" This time her voice was loud enough to drown a lion at full roar. People rose from their seats to see what the commotion was all about. Meanwhile, his left armpit joined the right one and now he felt like he was going to sink in his own body odor. He could smell his own anger and fear of the bitch.

He looked to his left and wasn't surprised to see James. A look of both shock and sympathy had replace his normally composed expression.

Poor dude must feel sorry for me.

He tried to smile at James, but it came out more like a grimace.

He said, "Well, you cut down my man days and resources! I estimated seven-hundred and that's exactly what I needed."

Margaret regained her composure. "This is not the first project you have failed to deliver. Your performance has been lousy lately, to say the least." Here we go. She was gonna lay it out all on the table. "You arrive late most of the time. And when everybody is still working, you decide you've had enough and disappear. Don't you think for one minute I hadn't noticed. And then, your deadlines suffer, and I am the one who has to explain this to the users."

With her voice lowered, the interest had been lost. Most of the idiots, who had nothing better to do, sat back down in their little cubicles like good little lambs. Fucking pathetic. It wasn't that they worked harder, they just knew how to ass-lick a little better.

Jarod could see that this was not going to end well. He tried to calm himself down. "Listen," he said. "It's not too late, and we still have two weeks. You give me one or two extra guys to help with the testing and I can still make it."

"Jarod, if I did have one or two extra guys, I would have given them to you in the first place."

Jarod shifted on his chair. He tried to sound confident. "I can make it. Come on. There must be a couple of people that aren't that busy right now."

"Fine," she said, her tone down a notch. "Let me see what I can do. But Jarod, no more coming in late, and when a project is late, you *do not* leave at six o'clock sharp. Okay? I'm going to help you out, so you had better not let me down."

Right. She was just trying to save her own ass because the head of IT was gonna come down on her faster than green grass through a goose.

"Okay," he replied like a good boy. "Let me know if you can find someone and in the meantime I'll try to get this project rolled out into production."

She threw him him a look of distaste and managed a one-eighty turn on her disproportional small feet that were amazingly able to support her hippo frame. She walked off, hippo butt wobbling, back to her bee-hive.

Jarod heard his phone ring.

Internal call.

He knew who it was.

He picked it up. "I'll see you at the car park, mate," he said into the receiver, not giving the caller a chance to introduce himself.

"Okay, dude," James replied. "Meet you there in five minutes. And make sure the bitch doesn't see you take off. Don't want to get you into any deeper shit than you already are. "

He hung up.

****

"So what the fuck was all that about?" James said, passing a cigarette to Jarod and lighting it up for him.

"Mate, well, you know, it's this bloody shimmer. I can't concentrate." Jarod took a deep drag. Nothing like the first hit. His muscles relaxed, and he welcomed the offending nicotine into his system. "Now I get it quite often at work, so that's also the reason why I always leave on time. I just don't wanna be in the office when it shows up. It just comes when it wants." He took another drag. "Shit mate, this is bad. This is the third project I fucked up, and the bitch has really got it in for me."

"Dude, maybe you should do what a doctor. Go and see a neurologist. Who knows, maybe you have some kind of tumor and it's affecting your eyes.

"Thanks a lot, mate! That makes me feel a lot better," Jarod said in despair.

"Don't get me wrong, dude! It's just that Andrew said it's not your eyes. I'm just trying to be practical here. You have to explore every avenue to find out what's really wrong. Even if it were a tumor, it doesn't mean it has to be malignant. You know what I'm saying?"

"Yea, I know...sorry, I know you're just trying to help." Jarod was tired. He wanted to give up. His whole life had been turned upside down because of this stupid shimmer. James was probably right though, he should go and see a neurologist. What harm could it do anyway?

But he was scared.

58

Scared that the neurologist would find nothing. Scared that there would be no explanation. Scared that he really was going crazy. But what about Mary? She has seen it too. How did that make any sense? What the fuck? It's not like they could share a tumor now, is it?

Jarod took one more drag and flicked his cigarette. He wanted another one. He looked up at James and smiled. His friend knew him so well. James pulled out a cigarette and lit it up for him with his own butt. "Mate, there is a reason why I don't think seeing a neurologist is gonna help. I know for a fact that it's not a tumor."

James took one last inhale, the tip of his cigarette reaching his finger tips. "What do you mean you know? What, are you a doctor now?"

"No, but, you know that kid, Mary, I was telling you about earlier with her grandma?"

"The one you met in the street?"

"Yeah, well, I went to her house. I wanted to see where they live and wanted to see if I could help."

"Okay, and?"

"I think Mary also saw the shimmer."

"What?" James's cigarette almost fell off his lips. "That's impossible! How the hell could you both see it? You told me it was some kind of headache, and you saw the wavy thing right? It doesn't sound like something that could be passed on. If it's your eyes or your brain, how you could possibly pass it on to the kid?"

"How the fuck do I know? All I know is that she saw it. Just like me. Her eyes saw the light, the shimmer. Even with her eyes closed, she could see it."

James looked dumbfounded. "That's really *weird*, dude."

Nothing made any sense anymore. Maybe one good thing though—if they both could see it, it definitely wasn't a tumor.

A car went passed. Wheels screeching on the smooth parking lot concrete floor. James watched it disappear and

59

said, "Dude, I think I may have an idea. I know it's a long shot, but at this stage I guess you've got nothing to lose anyway. Why don't you write a blog?"

"A blog? Why do I need a blog for?"

"Well, dude, if you have that kind of problem, and even that kid Mary, chances are that you two are not the only ones."

Jarod still couldn't get it. "Yeah, and?"

"Jesus!" said James slapping his forehead. "Do I have to draw you a picture or something? Someone out here might be able to shed some light! If you have a blog, other people will see it and maybe, who knows? Someone might know something…"

"Shit!" Jarod said. "You're right! It makes sense! If Mary and I can both see it, chances are quite high that we are not the only ones! "

Jarod smiled. Things might work out somehow. Thank God for James—genius. He took a last drag of his cigarette and flicked it to the ground. "Well, better get back to it, mate, or the bitch is gonna have my balls for breakfast."

CHAPTER 8

Jarod was at home staring at his computer screen—well, more like right through it. He looked at his watch. 20:45. He had stayed back at work till eight so the bitch wouldn't bitch. But enough was enough. No way he was going to stay overnight.

He wondered what he could put on his blog so that people would, at least, get an idea as to what was happening to him. Not exactly the easiest thing to describe without sounding like a complete moron.

"Okay, here we go," he said to himself. Talking to himself now? Was that a progression towards losing it? Who cared. He was halfway through losing it anyways. Maybe all the way.

His fingers stroked the keyboard, with the hope finding the right words. Then, after a minute, the keystrokes became sentences on the screen.

My name is Jarod Johnson. I'm forty two years old and work in a bank. I hate my job but I have to pay the rent. I have a girlfriend I love very much. I guess she loves me too...for now anyway. The reason I'm writing this blog is that I have a problem. To cut a long story short, it started a few weeks ago. Right at the corner of my eye, I can sometimes see a shimmer. Like a heat wave rising from the hot macadam that you would normally see on a very hot summer's day. It can be accompanied with a very sharp pain in my right eye and even when my eyes are closed, I can still see it. The shimmer (if I may call it that) seems to be more and more frequent. It's driving me crazy. I saw an optometrist and he seems to thinks that it's my mind. But I know what I'm seeing, and I know I'm not imagining it. It's there and it's real. As real as the hand that's attached to my arm.

Also, I met a kid. Her name is Mary. For some reason, I could feel a strong connection with her since the day we met. I went to see her at her house and guess what? She saw it too, she also saw the shimmer. What are the chances of that?

My life is being destroyed by this shimmer. I cannot meet deadlines at work. I think that if it continues like this, I'm going to lose my job. It's also affecting my relationship with my girlfriend. She thinks I'm having an affair, and this stupid shimmer always seems to come at the wrong time—if you know what I mean.

Please. I need help. Is there anyone out there who may have any idea as to what's happening to me? Does anyone else see a shimmer? I know I'm not crazy. Mary can also see it. And if she can, and I can, I'm sure someone else also can. Somewhere out there.

I need to know. It's getting worse. I'm desperate and really don't know what to do. I need to know what's happening to me before this shimmer takes over my life and destroys me.

Done! Jarod read through what he had typed. He hesitated for second and hit the 'return' key. Now, he just had to wait and hope someone out there had the same problem—not that he would wish it on anybody—but it would help his cause.

He needed a whiskey now and headed for the kitchen. Always seemed to help. He knew it wasn't the right time for it, but who cared. Some people even had a shot in their coffee for breakfast, right? Catalina would be here soon and she'd probably want one as well.

Just as the thought left his mind, he heard the keys rattle at the font door, and the door being pushed opened.

"Hi babe!" Good sign, she sounded cheerful. "Are you home?"

"Yes, honey!" he yelled out and raised the bottle of whiskey. "I'm getting a whiskey, you want one?"

"A bit early for me," she said and entered the kitchen.

How come she always smelled so good and managed to look so fresh? That was the thing about women in general though. No matter whether they had had a crappy day or not, they always managed to look as if their day had just begun. Well, except for the bitch—she looked more like she always just got out of bed. While guys, on the other hand, usually looked like shit at the end of the day.

Jarod felt a stir in his loin.

Okay… take it easy big boy, the night is still young.

She put her hands on her hips and swung her ass to the side. That little devious smirk he loved so much was playing on her lips. "Caught you again...buster!"

"Damn!" He felt the heat rising. "Am I that obvious?"

"You are not," she said and smiled, her eyes going south. "But he is..."

He looked down and yep, there *he* was. In all its glory. The tent was pretty obvious in his boxer shorts.

He looked back up, a little embarrassed and feeling the increasing pressure pushing against the front of his shorts. He smiled. "Lucky we don't work in the same office honey, otherwise I'd be walking around with a constant camping site."

"Guys... is that all you think about?" she asked, pretending to be annoyed but loving the attention. "I'm all hot and sweaty, my hair's a mess and my make up is running. And all you can think about is sex. I must look revolting. Shows you how desperate you are."

"Mmmm, just the way I like it honey. Office lady after a hard day's work. Total turn on. Want a massage?" he winked.

"Oh yeah? I know where this is heading." She took a few tantalizing steps towards him, and just before she reached him, she did a one-eighty so he could grab her from behind.

And he did.

He kissed her sensuous neck and pressed his manhood against her.

He loved that neck and he loved her smell. He could just stand there and smell her all night long.

Nothing wrong with a bit of sweat.

"Calm down," she moaned. "Let me have a shower first. You enjoy that whiskey and I promised I'll make it worth your wait."

She lingered a few more seconds in his arms and enjoyed the embrace and the soft kisses that moistened her neck, before she finally relented and headed towards the bathroom, giving him one more long sensual look. She made sure she removed her panties before she entered, looking back knowingly over her shoulder with a flirtatious smile.

She left them on the floor. As always. Had anyone ever died of lust? Because Jarod was starting to think that it could actually be possible. He was pretty sure that if he were to look in the dictionary for the word "TEASE", Catalina would be the first entry he would find.

He shook his head, trying to come back to his senses.

Finally having filled his glass, and having made sure it was a double, he settled himself on his favorite couch. That whiskey sure had a way to make you feel better.

And that shimmer had better not come back now.

It didn't.

After her shower, things had erected exponentially. And faster than you could pull a rabbit out of a hat, his clothes had magically disappeared and the magic was done right there and then—on the couch.

Now they lay in a heap on the floor. God only knew how they had ended up down there— panting, but satisfied.

"Wow..." Her voice was but a whisper, still hoarse from the orgasmic squeal. "I wonder if the neighbors heard us."

"Who cares," he replied and tried to catch his breath. "At least they don't need to buy porn. They've got live porn right here next door."

"Ha, ha, ha," she laughed out a bit too loud. "You are incorrigible Mr. Johnson...but maybe that's why I like you."

She got up on one elbow and looked at his face. He opened his eyes, a frown forming on his brow.

"Like?" he questioned, looking hurt. "Not, love?"

"Mmmm," she pondered and pinched her lips together. "Such a big word, you know. You can't just throw it around, babe. You have to mean it."

"I do!"

"You do what?" she toyed, her eyebrows rising.

"Love you."

That brought a smile to her face. She was beautiful when she smiled. In fact, she was beautiful even when she didn't smile.

"That's sweet, babe...you're sweet," she said. But she wouldn't go any further and he didn't want to push her. Was her love diminishing because of this damn shimmer? Didn't she say that she loved him before? He wasn't sure now. Had she really ever said it? Or maybe *he* had always been the one?

Jarod hoped he wasn't losing her. He couldn't imagine his life without her. And yes, he did believe it was love he felt for her, he wasn't just saying it, he meant it. And not just because she was the best sex he had ever had, by far, but because she was...her.

And you know what? That was just fine...

CHAPTER 9

Mary pressed the green answering button on her new cell phone and raised the phone to her ear. "Whaii?"

"Mary," Jarod said. "It's me, Jarod. I'm at the gate. Are you home? Could you open the gate for me please?"

"Jarod! Yes! Me home. Wait, me open gate now."

So cheerful. Guess she doesn't get visitors.

The smell was still there. It was an unpleasant mixture of shit mingled with rotten eggs thrown in for good measure. And yep, as sure as he took a piss this morning, the good ol' human/dog urine paddle was still decorating the foyer two floors down, making him 'jump over paddles'—*oh you are a funny one Jarod*—of piss.

To his right was the never-emptied, overflowing bin. Litter spewing out of it like a child vomiting his last meal on the car seat.

After what seemed like an eternity, and he guessed anything more than a minute would feel like that in here, the steel gate finally opened with a rusty creak that was begging for WD40.

Mary's face appeared. If her smile were any wider, she would've had no problem getting an audition for the horror movie 'Fright Night'. Mary was happy to see him—no doubt about that.

He followed her down the dark, narrow hallway and with an expert kick to the bottom of the flimsy entrance door, followed by a push and a grunt, Mary expertly opened the door to her nest.

Given the size of the place, Jarod could only think of it as a nest—barely enough for a couple of chicks.

Jarod said, "How have you been Mary? How is school? Anything new? How is Pawpaw?" He settled himself on the left cane chair.

Mary installed her skinny self on the right one. She looked at him, mouth half- opened as if ready to catch a fish. But not a sound came out.

Jarod frowned at the mute reply, then realized it was probably too much at once. "Sorry, Mary! Okay, okay. One question at a time. Let's start again. How have you been Mary?"

This time, her mouth opened wider and her smile reappeared. "I very good Jarod. And you?"

"I'm okay, Mary," he sighted. "I've seen better days, but I have seen worse also…"

Her eyebrows shot up. "Better? Worse?"

Jarod didn't feel like explaining. "Never mind. I'm good… thanks."

This wasn't going to be easy. It was difficult to have a conversation when you had to re-explain everything. "How is school? Good?"

"School good," she said and smiled. "Me had test Thursday and me had seventy eight on one-hundred. Me happy because me not study many."

"Study *much*, Mary. You study *much*, not many, because you can't count it."

She scratched her head and twisted her mouth. "Oh, yes! Teacher told me that! That why my friend laugh when me say study many!"

Jarod smiled. Poor girl. Well, another one on his checklist. *Teach Mary basic English grammar.*

"You didn't study much? How come? You don't like to study?"

"Oh. No, me love study. Just me see more and more—how you say?"

"Shimmer?" Jarod said, almost hoping but knowing it was wrong to hope.

"Yes! Shimmer! Me see more and more. Now everyday see shimmer. Me see shimmer *a lot.* So hard for study. Even school, me sometime see shimmer."

Jarod was horrified. This seemed to be a lot more frequent than him. He saw it often, but definitely not everyday.

"Wow!" he said. "That's bad Mary! Damn!" He sat back and thought for a minute.

Mary looked at him and smiled.

He looked up again, crossed his fingers and leaning forward. "Okay, when you say everyday, do you mean like once a day or twice a day? More? How many times, Mary?"

She looked up at the ceiling, a deep furrow forming between her eyes. "Sometime one time, sometime two time and when me have test me have more."

Stress seems to be making it worse.

But hang on—that didn't make sense. He remembered having had a few incidences of the shimmer appearing whilst having sex with Cat. Was sex considered stressful? Well, he guessed, physically? Probably. "How bad was it. Mary? Did you have it *while* in class?"

"Yes," she replied. "Two time at school at lesson. Have big headache but me say nothing. Me don't want look stupid."

Jarod rubbed the subtle growth on his chin. "And did you see anything? You remember last time? You told me that you saw a shadow."

"Me did! Me saw shadow. Like someone walk pass. One time look like woman and one time look like man."

Jarod was stunned. It appeared Mary was one step ahead of him as far as the shimmer was concerned. What was going on? How could this be happening to both of them? What were the chances of that? There seemed to be no answer.

He looked at Mary. The poor girl looked tired. He felt tired himself. The shimmer was taking over their lives—over and over again and there was nothing they could do about it.

"I saw it too," he finally said. "I also saw a shadow. But I wasn't sure what it was at first. But now that you mention it, it did seem to be a person walking past. But it wasn't clear. It was like watching someone walk past through a very dense fog."

Mary frowned. "What is fog?".

"Mist. You know, sometimes when you go out and it's like you're in the clouds? You can't see much in front of you and everything looks like shadows."

"Yes," Mary said. "Is like that! Like fog! Hard to see but can still see woman walk pass."

Jarod was wondering what it could be. Were they seeing something that no one else could? What could it be? Why them? There were many more questions than answers. In fact, there were no answers—only questions. Jarod hoped someone would leave an answer on his blog. Even if not the right answer, or maybe even something crazy, would be better than what they had so far. Nothing.

"Mary," he said, "I know that this is bad and we don't know what's going on. But trust me ,okay? I'm going to find out what's happening and as soon as I know anything, you'll be the first one to know. I promise."

"Okay," Mary said, lost in her own thoughts, "thank you Jarod. Me don't like shimmer. Shimmer is bad and give me bad headache. Me is scared, Jarod."

Jarod felt bad, almost as if it were his fault she was also suffering from the shimmer. She was too young, to frail for this. He leaned forward and took her small hand in his. She seemed lost, afraid, like a little sparrow away from its nest. He gave it a squeeze.

"Mary. I'd like you to do something for me. This may be a way to find out something, but best of all, to try to at least to have some control over this thing."

She didn't let go of his hand. "Okay Jarod," she said. "What can me do.?"

"Every time you see the shimmer, I want you to remember and write down what you were doing before it occurred. And maybe also what you were eating and drinking. Anything at all. I'm trying to see if we have a pattern here. Something that might trigger it. This way, maybe, just maybe, we can have some kind of control over it."

"Okay," she said. "Me do this. Me write on paper and when you come next time, me show you."

"That's great, Mary." At least they had a plan. "I hope that we can control it, even if we can't stop it." Jarod let go of her hand and got up. He was tired. "I need to go, Mary. I have things to do." He lied and moved towards the door.

"Oh, okay," Mary said and looked up at him, a disappointed expression on her face. "Me is very happy you come Jarod. Me always happy you come. Please, if you like Jarod, come more." She was almost begging.

Jarod felt a lump in his throat. He felt so bad and guilty leaving Mary cooped up in this hell-hole.

"Hey listen," he said and looked at his watch, just for show. "I have a little bit of time. Why don't you come down with me and we can grab something to eat. Would you like that?"

Mary's beautiful smile re-emerged like a rainbow after a storm.

Jarod's heart missed a beat and melted. He reached out and she took his hand.

"Yes Jarod, me like that very many. Oops, sorry, very much!"

Together they ventured down the dark, damp stairway to be greeted by a bright, blue sky and a warm sunny day.

CHAPTER 10

As soon as he arrived home, he went straight for his computer.

While it was booting up, Jarod walked into the kitchen, grabbed a glass from the sink and poured himself a double finger of his favorite guy—Johnny Walker. Whoever had invented whiskey was a fucking genius. He let the golden liquid warm his chest while he inhaled its smoky aroma.

He sat in front of the screen and slowly sipped his drink. It seemed to take forever but finally he made it to his blog. There were three messages. He opened the first one.

"Jarod, it seems like you are experiencing some kind of hallucination. Maybe a doctor can help. Could you be taking some kind of drug or medication at the moment? I use to take some stuff, if you know what I mean, and I also started to see things. These…"

Okay, he had read enough. This reply wasn't going to be any help at all. "Thanks for nothing," he muttered. "Sorry to disappoint you but I'm not into the hard stuff."

He couldn't be bothered replying and decided to check out the other two messages.

The second message was also bullshit about a possible brain tumor that must be affecting his vision. Well, that could have worked, maybe, if Mary happened to have a brain tumor as well. Did these guys actually read his blog before they replied? Was little Mary also supposed to be on drugs or have a brain tumor?

Right, well, this wasn't much good so far. Third time lucky? He hoped that the last reply would make more sense, or at least give him something to shoot for.

"Jarod. My name is Jim Andrews. I'm a quantum physicist and I may have a theory as to what may be wrong with you, or more likely, what you may be seeing. It's a bit complicated to explain in here so could you please email me at j.andrews@gmail.com and give me your details? I'll call you back."

"Wow!" Jarod leaned back on his chair. That seemed to be going in a totally different direction. Wasn't quantum mechanics linked to how things worked at quantum level? He had heard something, somewhere that the laws of physics we are familiar with are very different at the quantum level. But what did that have to do with him?

He clicked on "REPLY".

"Dear Jim, very interested in what you have to say. My number is 93349154. Please call me ASAP. I'm desperate for an answer—no matter how crazy it may sound."

His finger hesitated for a fraction of a second and he pressed the ENTER key. With a swoosh, the message instantly traveled to its recipient.

He sat there, taking another sip. Waiting. He looked at his watch—18:36. The cursor was blinking endlessly. Waiting. He too another sip, listening to the ice-cubes clinging together—18:37.

Did he really think that Jim, a quantum physicist, wouldn't have anything better to do than to call him ASAP? The guy must be busy on some research. What did a quantum physicist

73

do anyway? How did he help the world? Or more importantly, how could he help him?— 18:39.

"This is bullshit. I ain't gonna seat here and wait forever," he sighed. "Time for a hot shower and maybe another shot of whiskey to calm my nerves."

Just as soon as Jarod stood up, his phone rang. The number showed "UNKNOWN". Jarod pressed the answer key and put the receiver to his ear.

"Err... hello?" he hesitated—hoping.

"Hello? May I speak to Mr. Jarod Johnson please?" The voice at the other end sounded cracked, old. That meant he was probably experienced and knew what he was on about — right?

"Yes, this is Jarod speaking."

"Right, well I'm calling about that problem you have mentioned on your blog, what you referred to as the shimmer."

"Okay, yes," Jarod said. "I'm still having it. In fact it's been getting more frequent and also the headaches have been getting more intense. Especially behind the right eye."

"I see," replied Dr. Andrews. "Well Mr. Johnson—"

"—Jarod is fine Dr. Andrews.".

"Jarod. Right! And you can call me Jim." Jarod heard Dr. Andrews taking a deep breath as if he were about to start a speech. "Jarod, as mentioned in my reply, I'm a quantum physicist which means that I study and deal with quantum mechanics. Do you know what that entails Mr. Johnson— Jarod?"

Jarod took a seat. Looked like it was going to be a long conversation. "I guess it means you study science at a quantum level? Like really, really small?"

"Yes, you could say that. But to make it clearer, let me tell you a little bit more."

74

"Okay." Jarod couldn't imagine how this could have anything to do with him but at this stage, he was willing to be patient and see what the man had to say.

Jim continued, "Particles at that level behave very differently than they do at our level—or should I say size. In fact, the laws of physics as we know them do not apply."

"Okay," Jarod said. "But what has that got to do with me?"

"Just be patient with me, Jarod. I'll get there soon. Let me explain a bit more first. It will make it easier to understand. In fact, it may have a lot more do to with you than you think. Theoretically speaking, of course."

"At this stage, I'm ready for anything." He welcomed another sip, of the now-almost-empty glass, channel it's way down and he felt his nerve endings relax. "Anything that may make some sense out of this shimmer that's destroying my life."

"Okay," Jim said impatiently. "Let me explain and then maybe you'll have an idea of what *may* be happening to you. To begin with Jarod, have you even heard of multi-universes?"

Jarod frowned and bit his lower lip. "Yes. I think I have...It's like parallel universes?"

"Well, yes, in a way. But more like on top of one-another. Like superimposed. Basically, multi-universes is only a theory based on quantum mechanics. It's telling us that our universe is not the only one. In fact, it's telling us that there is an infinite number of universes all around us. I won't get into the quantum mechanics and string theory that have led us to this theory but basically, since quantum mechanics does not obey the natural laws of physics, particles that exist at that level tend to take on different arbitrary forms. For example, photons, which are tiny particles of light, can also act as particles of wave."

Jarod started to feel a bit confused. "Sorry doc, you got me a bit lost there."

"To put it simply, it would be just like you were human one minute whilst someone was looking at you and if he were to turn around and look at you again, you would have changed to a gaseous form. I know it's a bit confusing, but with me so far?"

"Okay." He was kind of getting it but also wondered where this was headed.

"This is called the uncertainty theory," Jim continued. "And essentially, when observing a quantum matter, we inadvertently affect its behavior. Meaning that we can never be sure of its attributes, like velocity and location. In a nutshell, it means that all quantum particles do not exist in one state or another, but in fact... in all possible states at once."

"I see," Jarod said, still a bit baffled. "But again, what's that got to do with me?" His patience was starting to wear thin.

"We are getting there, Jarod. Please bear with me a little longer."

Patience, thought Jarod. That was a joke. He had already been more than patient. In fact, so much so, that he was seriously starting to run out of it. "I'm sorry," he said nevertheless. "Please continue."

"Thank you. Right. So since we are able to change the state of quantum particles by simply observing them, it means that every single quantum possibility becomes a possibility in some reality. This, in turn, creates a parallel universe, or in fact, parallel universes. But normally we have no way of seeing them even-though we are constantly in contact with them. Every moment of your life and every decision you make is creating a split version of your now-self into an infinite number of future selves. All of which are totally unaware of each-another. All of which continue their lives whence they have just began and continue them on a totally different path. Think of it as a train track splitting into two directions and taking on two different paths. But all of these multi-universes do not actually split; we could actually say that they coexist since there is only one wave function. So, in fact, these separated, yet very close universes, interfere with each other yielding the bizarre quantum behavior that we observe."

There was a pause. That was a lot to take in. Jarod tried to wrap his head around what Dr. Andrews had just said. He wanted another whiskey. Maybe later.

"Wow," he said after a moment's reflection. "That's quite a lot to digest. I kinda got it, even though it seems a bit far-fetched... but, what are you actually trying to tell me? And... I still can't see what any of this has to do with me."

Jarod heard the excitement building up in Dr. Andrews' voice. "What I'm telling you, Jarod, is I believe that you are able to see, if I may use such a word, into one or more of these parallel universes!"

"What? That's impossible! If what you say is true—and that's a *big* if, didn't you say yourself that we have no way of seeing them?"

"Yes," Jim said as if talking to a small child. "You are absolutely right, Jarod. I did say that. That's true for most of us."

He needed that whiskey now—more than ever. "Could you please hold on for one second? I'll be right back?"

"Sure, Jarod, take your time"

He put down the receiver and headed back to the kitchen. He poured himself another double. *Screw it,* he thought, and made it a triple. He felt the warmth spread and warm him inside. Light-headed, Jarod made his way back and picked up the phone again.

"Yellooooo…" he slurred. "Still here? Sorry to keep you waiting."

Shit, he was getting drunk.

"Yes, yes. And not a problem Jarod," replied Dr. Andrews. "Are you okay? I know that this must be quite a shock for you and in fact, I wouldn't blame you if you suddenly decided to hang up and tell me that I'm full of it."

Jarod's grip tightened on his cell phone, his finger tips becoming white. "No! No, please." he said desperately. "I don't think you are crazy or anything! Hell, to be honest, this is the only explanation, no matter how crazy it sounds, that seems to make any sense out of all this."

He relaxed, the whiskey having finally done its job. His voice became a resigned sigh. "This whole shimmer thing has been driving me crazy and maybe this multi-universe theory is what I need to hear. I need an answer. In fact, the more you are telling me, the more I'm starting to believe it."

"Okay, Jarod, I'm glad to see that we are on the same page." Jarod could hear a sense of relief in his voice. He needed to know more however.

"Hang on," he said. "What makes you think, this is what's happening to me? What's the link?"

"Let me explain about the shimmer the way you described it, and how I have made the connection. The fact that not only you but also that child can see it—what's her name again?"

"Mary..."

"Yes, Mary...so. yes, the fact Mary can also see it means you both have the same symptoms, and you both have seen the other side."

"You mean the shadows we saw are part of another universe?"

"Yes, exactly, that's what I believe. But, you must understand theories of parallel universes are just that; theories, and so is my assessment derived from them. However, there has been other cases, although very few and dissimilar to yours and Mary, to support my explanation."

"Cases?" Jarod was stupefied, half hoping the scientist's reasoning would help him. "Do you mean there are others like Mary and myself?"

"In a way, yes," Dr. Andrews said. "But not exactly."

Jarod felt the familiar wetness spreading under his right armpit. "What do you mean not exactly?"

"I mean, cases where one individual would suddenly, out of nowhere, say that he was having a totally different life than the one he remembers. As if waking up from a dream. Except that the dream wasn't a dream. To that person, the dream and the memories are real."

"How is that possible?" Jarod sat down and drained the remainder of his whiskey.

"A few years back a man believed he had a completely different past, and that the present he was currently in was totally new to him. Many people he remembered from his past did not in fact exist right now, and people he knew in the present, many of them, were previously unknown to him previously. It was as if he had *jumped* from another parallel universe into ours. All he could remember was *his* universe—*his* previous world."

"Wow," mumbled Jarod, more to himself than to Jim. Could that be possible? Could someone actually jump from another universe into ours? The whole theory seemed crazy, but then anything was possible. Doesn't everything we don't know or don't understand sound crazy? Like when we discovered electricity? The telegraph? Even when we finally realized that the world was round and that we were not going to fall off the edge? Just because we don't understand something doesn't mean that it doesn't exist.

Jarod said, "But why me? If what you are saying is true, why me? I'm just an average guy, living an average life. And what about Mary?"

"Jarod, I don't think that we can pick and choose who we are and what we are capable of. When, for example, a man gets struck by lighting, that man didn't choose for this to happen to him. Was there something special about him that had attracted lightning? No. Well, maybe you and Mary share something in common. Something rare. Maybe even something unique. Something that can't be explained. And who knows, maybe there are others. All I can say for sure Jarod, is that if all this is what I think it is, then you have a gift. Both you and Mary."

"A gift?" Jarod's voice picked up volume. "Seriously? More like a curse! This shimmer is destroying my life, and you should see what it's doing to Mary. She is only a child for God's sake! She is scared!" Jarod felt anger mounting —the alcohol was losing its soothing effect. "This shimmer. is going to cost me my girlfriend! My job! Everything! And you call *this* a gift?"

"Now, now, Jarod," Dr. Andrews said calmly. "I understand how upsetting it must be, but honestly, you do have a gift. You are seeing something that probably only a handful of people in this world are able to see. You, my friend, are seeing something that no-one is supposed to see."

Jarod tried to relax. It wasn't the doctor's fault after all, he was only trying to help. "Well, honestly, doc, I would rather not have a special *gift*, given the choice. I'd rather have a normal life. What's the point of this anyway? Even if what you are saying is true, what's the point of me seeing a parallel universe?"

This was ridiculous. Even far-fetched—and Jarod couldn't believe he was starting to fall for this. But, in the end, losers couldn't be choosers and it seemed the scientist's theory was the only one that made any sense at all up till now. As much as he hated to admit it, he had to wonder if it actually was possible.

"What about Mary?" he asked. "You said only a handful of people may have this *gift*. Then how do you explain Mary? What are the chances of two people having it *and* having met? I think I'd probably have more chance of winning the lottery two consecutive weeks."

"It may be, and of course don't just take my word for it, that you and Mary's meeting was not a coincidence. You see, everything has a purpose—a motive. Assuming you and Mary do have some connection in a parallel universe could mean you also share a bond in our world, an invisible link of some sort. Right now, we are only scratching at the surface of quantum mechanics and trying to make sense out of it is, similarly to those who tried to understand electricity a thousand years ago. One day we may know more, but in the meantime, there are more questions than answers. All we have at this stage are theories and speculations."

A connection? Could that be what it was? Could Mary and him be somehow connected in another universe? Were they meant to bump into each other? Is that why Jarod had instantly felt this special bond with Mary when they had first met?

"Okay," Jarod said. He had heard enough for now and needed to digest the information he'd just been given. "I really want to thank you, Dr. Andrews. I know I might have sounded a bit ungrateful but I'm not. As far-fetched as it may seem to me, you explanation is, in fact, the only one making any sense to me right now. I know the shimmer is not just something in my head, but something real—so real in fact, even Mary is displaying the same symptoms. And that can't be a mental problem."

He picked up the glass. The ice had melted. He swallow the watery remaining whiskey in one gulp. His head spun slightly. The numbness felt good. He wished it were all a dream.

"You are more than welcome," Dr. Andrews said. "Please, do let me know if you see anything more, by which I mean, *anything* more substantial. On my side, I'll do my best to find out about the shimmer and maybe try to find other similar cases to you and Mary."

Jarod closed his eyes. "Okay, you'll be the first one to know, promise. And again, many thanks for responding. You don't know how much it means for me to know I'm not crazy, theoretically speaking of course. Anyway, it's something to hold on to."

"Yes, it is, Jarod. Yes it is," reassured Jim. "Keep in touch, okay? I'm sorry but I need to get back to work now. Make sure to let me know should anything change."

"Will do," Jarod said. "Bye Dr. Andrews. And thanks again."

"Bye, Jarod. Talk to you soon."

Jarod heard Dr. Andrews' phone make a click as it found its cradle. He put his cell phone down as well. He was dumbfounded. He had pretty much been ready for anything—but parallel universes? That was a bit more than he was able to swallow.

He stood up.

"I need another whiskey," he said to himself out loud.

And before he knew it, the bottle lay empty on the coffee table and Jarod was lying on his favorite couch, having fitful dreams of parallel universes, the whiskey glass laying on the floor, barely touching his fingertips.

CHAPTER 11

"Jesus Christ! Not now!"

Jarod was sitting at his desk. It was there again. Couldn't be timed any worse. If he didn't finish his Functional Specification today, he would be in deep trouble.

Maybe if he could just try to ignore it for a while. Just enough to finish this damn spec. But ignoring it proved as impossible as running a marathon with a stone in your shoe. Every step, it was there to remind you that no matter what you did, you were bound to fail—it was inevitable.

Though his eyes were closed, he could still see it. It was taunting him—annoying the hell out of him.

And now the headache.

What started off as an almost indiscernible pulse was now developing into a jackhammer-pounding migraine compounded by the fucking shimmer.

"How is the spec going, Jarod?"

"What... wha...what?" He fluttered open his eyes and turned around. She was right there—the bitch. Now what?

"Having a nice sleep, are we Mr. Johnson?" She smiled sarcastically. She leaned on his desk, her fat stumps, that are mistaken for hands, resting heavily upon his paperwork.

Another minute, and my fucking desk is gonna collapse.

The pain was now becoming unbearable, like knives being driven in and out of his cranium. "I wasn't slee...ping," he finally managed to utter through clenched teeth, every syllable sending a sharp jab into his brain and making him cringe. "I have this *really* bad head...ache. And—"

Her mouth puckered outward, making her look like a puffer-fish. "I don't want to hear anything about any bad headaches or any excuses Mr. Johnson," she cut in. "I want this spec on my desk before you go home. And I don't care if it means that you have to stay here overnight."

He could barely see her now. The shimmer was taking over. She was barely visible though his left eye, while his right eye was trying to created a mirage out of his terminal like heat waves rising from an overheated desert soil.

"It's not an excuse, bitch!"

The words came out before he had the chance to hold them back. Shit! Had he just called her a bitch right to her face?

She took a step back, the shock showing all over her inflated face. The small hole that stood for a mouth was opened like an O. The puffer-fish impression even more apparent. Her eyes narrowed. "What did you just call me?"

Fuck, fuck, fuck! She had heard him. Fuck! "Nothing... I didn't call you anything," he mumbled.

"No, no, no, Mr. Johnson." Her voice was rising exponentially and like metal to a magnet, heads started to turn. "I have definitely heard you calling me a *bitch*," she continued, accentuating the 'B' to make sure everyone had heard it.

Damn it! Can she be any louder?

"Look, calm down," he said, knowing he had more chance to rationalize with a mule than her. "It wasn't you. I mean... I do have a bad headache, and I didn't know what I was saying. It just...came out. I'm sorry ,okay?"

She leaned forward. "Sorry? Well I'm sorry also Mr. Johnson, because sorry isn't going to cut it." Her voice was still loud—too loud. She was doing this on purpose. He knew it. She wanted to make sure everyone could hear her. Jarod looked around—they did, as sure as he was sitting here smelling his own nervous perspiration. "Not only are you behind on your schedule, but then, you have the audacity to disrespect me. Thus, I will *personally* make sure that HR hears about this." She looked around and turned back to Jarod. She smiled, her voice lower now. "And I've got plenty of witnesses it seems."

Jarod couldn't believe this was happening. The patch under his right arm had now grown to reach all the way down to his waist. "What? Seriously?" He didn't even want to think what would happen if HR found out. "Come on," he pleaded. "There's no need for that surely. It just... blurted out. I... I was tired. I have a major headache. It... just popped out from nowhere. I mean, I didn't even know it was you." That sounded like bullshit and he knew it.

Was that a smile? A Goddamn smile? Shit! The bitch was actually enjoying this! There was no way in hell she was gonna let him get away with it! She didn't even give a shit about being called a bitch, she knew she was one anyway. She was out to get him and this was her ticket. The bitch was out for revenge. Jarod realized this was a lost cause. He didn't have anything to lose anymore.

He took a deep breath. "You know what?" he said, now getting to his feet to make sure that the bitch wouldn't be able to look down on him. "I'll deny it. Bloody go ahead and tell HR. I'll just deny it. Your word against mine." His face was only a few inches from hers now.

There was a moment when her lips quivered. He thought he had won. But, her smile came back. Her disgusting, fucking puffer-fish smile.

"Oh really?" she said slowly, her head swiveling around to take a good look at the heads that were peering over the partitions.

Jarod spotted James. His mouth was half opened. His eyes were saying *what the fuck are you doing mate?*—imploring him to stop.

But Jarod was pissed. He was screwed anyway. Not only by the fucking shimmer but also by this bitch. Funny, somehow the shimmer was starting to fade. Maybe the ugly bitch scared it away. He couldn't help but smile at that thought.

"Fuck it, you know what? *Fuck it*!" he said.

Her eyes almost popped out of her head. "Wha... what?" she chocked.

"You heard me!" Wow! This felt *really* good!. "Fuck it! I said. Do what you wanna do, I don't give a flying fuck. I'm sick of your shit, and I'm not gonna take your crap anymore."

He grabbed the specs on impulse, rose them right up to her face and crumbled them in his fist. His face red, his hand shaking., he brought his face an extra inch closer to hers. She took half a step back but her bitchy attitude wouldn't let her go any further. He could see she was shaking. In response, he took a full step forward.

"Yes," he whispered, just loud enough for her to hear. "You heard me right the first time. You are a *bitch* and trust me, I'm not the only one who thinks so."

Her face was a display of shock. Wait a minute! Was that a tear forming at the corner of her eye! Sure looked like it. This was so totally worth it. Let's see if he could get that tear to come right out.

"No one here likes you," he continued. Now, it was his turn to smile. *Might as well go all the way.* "Everyone thinks you are lazy and you only stay back to look good. You don't do shit and expect your team to work their asses off for you."

Almost there—the tear.

Almost there.

One last blow and she is down. "Just because you don't have a life doesn't mean that you have to take it out on us."

She stared at him, too shocked to say anything. She looked like a wax figure, frozen in time.

"Yes, Margaret, you are a bitch. You know it, I know it—we both know it." BINGO! The fucking tear finally found its way down her over-inflated left cheek. Oh, the bliss! Revenge was sweet. And you know what? The shimmer was gone! He had found the cure! The bitch was the cure! Who would have known? She did have some use after all.

"You... you…" she blurted out.

"You... you what?" he cut in.

"You... can't talk to me like that," she said, trying to recompose herself.

"Like hell I can't!" This time it was his voice that was rising —and so what? He couldn't care less. It had gone too far anyway. He looked around and made sure sure everyone was still there. "And you know what? I should have done this a long time ago."

"But..."

Jarod saw a movement behind her. Someone was heading his way. He didn't care. Fuck it...

It was James.

He grabbed Jarod's arm at the elbow.

"Come on dude, let's go for a fag," he said, matter-of-factly.

Jarod resisted.

James said, "Please dude, it's not worth it."

Jarod turned to him. The anger was dissipating. He turned back and gave the bloated face one last despising look. "Yea fuck it." he said, staring into her eyes.

A second tear emerged. It felt so good. He felt like an asshole, but it felt *sooo* good. He looked at her up and down, his lip rising in disgust. "*She* is not worth it."

He let go of the crumbled spec and it landed noiselessly right between her legs—exactly where it belonged.

"Let's go," James insisted.

He let James lead the way, ignoring all the eyes like daggers on his back.

****

The parking lot was quiet at this time of the day. James lit two fags and handed one to Jarod. "What the fuck, dude?" he said without even taking the time to enjoy his first drag. "What the fuck? Are you nuts?"

Jarod closed his eyes for a minute. He inhaled the nicotine and felt it working into his system. Killing a few brain cells on a path to a slow but satisfying self-destruction.

After a few seconds, he opened them back up and excelled the blue smoke into a cloud that would merge with the air as innocently as a cancer forming deep inside his lungs. But hey, who gave a shit anyways.

"Mate," he said finally. "I've had enough of this bitch. She deserves everything she got, and she's had it coming for a long time as far as I'm concerned. It's about time someone stood up to her."

James shook his head. "Dude, I *know* she is a bitch, but come on, don't you think you went a bit too far? Shit! she is still your boss."

"So? What is she gonna do? Sack me?" Jarod shrugged.

She needs me. No way she'll have the balls. Balls…yeah, she probably has some anyway.

"Yes," James said, "she is going to make sure your head sits on a platter. She hates you as much as you hate her, and I'm sure she's been waiting for an opportunity like this for a long time."

Jarod swallowed. He took a drag and tried to sound confident. "No way, she wouldn't dare. Who the hell is gonna finish her stupid specs and her stupid project?"

James's eyebrows narrowed. "What? You think you are indispensable? Dude, there are plenty of project managers who could take your project quicker than you could take a shit. Anyone with half a brain and some credit card knowledge could take over."

"Wow! Thanks a lot! And no, I don't think they could, it's already way behind schedule."

"Right!" James said. "It *is* already behind schedule. And you know what that means don't you?"

"What?" Jarod said, his confidence starting to crumble.

"It means she doesn't give a shit anymore. You, getting the flick is gonna be a damn good excuse for her to delay the project to the next release without her getting the blame. You gonna be her scapegoat, buddy."

Jarod wasn't feeling so good anymore. The consumed tobacco reached his fingers tips, the burning sensation making him drop his cigarette absently. He said, "Shit, are you sure?"

Was he really going to lose his job? Not only the shimmer but now this? He knew that that quick temper of his was gonna get him in trouble one day. What the hell was he gonna do? What about Catalina? For sure she would be pissed and no way she was going to support his sorry ass.

"Mate," Jarod said, "maybe you're right. Maybe I did go too far. What am I gonna do?"

James blew out a breath. "Let me think, dude."

"Maybe I could deny everything! Like tell them I never called her a bitch! I don't know, maybe I could have said that I had... an itch! Yeah, that's it! And the bitch misunderstood!"

"Forget it, dude," James said and threw his cigarette butt in a puddle of water. "She has enough witnesses to fill up a grand stadium."

Jarod tossed his own butt and starred at it as it sizzled its last breath. "Fuck, you're right." His eyes looked at James like a lost puppy. "I'm so fucked!"

CHAPTER 12

Jarod looked at his watch—3am. He knew he had had one too many but he needed to clear his head. He was most probably going to lose his job; not just for calling Margaret a bitch, but also for missing more than one deadline.

He stood by the front door of his home and rummaged through his pockets for the keys—he couldn't remember which pocket they were in. Finally he felt them in his left pocket and removed them between his thumb and index finger. His head was spinning. He slowly and deliberately inserted the master key into the keyhole, making sure that's it wouldn't rattle—the last thing he wanted to do was to wake up Catalina.

Slowly he turned it clockwise. The click it made upon disengaging the locking mechanism was loud enough, in Jarod's mind, to wake the whole neighborhood. *Why do things you never even notice during the day always seem so much louder at night?*

After what seemed like an eternity, the door was unlocked. and with Jarod's shoulder against it, it slowly creaked open. Hopefully she would still be asleep.

He hadn't even thought of an excuse as to why he was coming home at this ungodly hour. And to make matters worse, his cell phone had run out of battery over five hours ago and he was fucked if he could remember her number. Did anyone actually remember numbers now? Why would you? It was in your cell phone—like the rest of your life.

He stepped in and his eyes focused on the light streaming out from the bedroom's opened door. *Shit!* She was still awake—awake and probably pissed as hell. Shit! Shit! Shit! Fuckerdifuckfuck!!

He cringed as the wooded floor creaked—no way she would have missed that.

Well…might as well get it over and done with.

He slowly made his way towards the bedroom. He felt like he was going to his own execution—dead man walking.

"Hi, babe," he called out, not too loud, trying to sound as sober as he could. "Sorry I'm bit late honey!" Two more steps and he would reach the electric chair. "I was just out for…" one more step.. "a fe…"

Zero.

Her look was enough to stop him dead in his tracks. He saw pain and anger. Her lower eye lids were so puffy that she looked liked a boxer who had just gone twelve rounds with Mike Tyson. Jarod swallowed, still feeling the remains of beer lingering in his saliva.

Shit, as if one argument hadn't been enough for one day.

"Why didn't you call?" she said, her voice cold enough to freeze alcohol.

"Babe," he struggled. "I'm sorry. I meant to call you but my phone was dead. And I… you know, had a few and… and I didn't realize the time. I'm so—"

"—Who is she?"

"Who? What?" What the hell was she talking about? And then he understood. "Oh, come on…you don't think?"

Her face was stone cold. "No, I don't think, Jarod, I know," she said through clenched teeth.

Jarod looked down and saw her hands squeezed into fists.

"Babe, please," he said with sincerity, "it's not what you think at all. I just had a bad day and—"

"—I don't want to hear it!" she screamed. She stood up and took a step closer to him. Jarod also took a step forward but the look she gave him put a stop to his forward momentum like a brick wall.

"Fuck you Jarod! After all I've given you! I was actually starting to love you! Stupid me!" She turned around and sat on the edge of the bed.

Jarod wanted to hold her, to tell her she got it all wrong.

"God I was so stupid," she continued, her voice now but a whisper. "I was so stupid to even think that you were any different from all the other guys. You are such a fucking asshole. And you know what? You are right, it's not your fault." Jarod frowned. "It's mine…" She sobbed, a tear rolling down her cheek. Her body was shaking, her voice quivering. "It's mine… for loving you…"

Jarod felt a lump in his throat. He could hardly speak.

"Come on," he struggled. "I swear—"

She snapped back. Her eyes turned to meet his. He could see the hurt, the disappointment. He could see the *hate*. "Fuck you! Fuck you! And go back to your whore!"

"Babe," he said, trying again to move towards her. But before he knew it, she was right in front of him, her hands on his chest. She pushed him away and Jarod lost his balance and his back hit the hallway wall.

Before he had time to react, she slammed the bedroom door so hard, that a piece of plaster fell off the door frame. He heard the click, he was locked out. He let himself sink to the ground.

"Babe, come on! Why are you doing this? I told you I've had a bad day and went for a couple of drinks! And then my phone went dead." No sound. "Babe! Please! Open the door! I swear there's no one. I love you babe! You only!"

He heard banging coming from the bedroom. "Fuck you! Fuck you and your bitch! Fuck you and your shimmer! Or whatever the fuck it is. I'm sick of this shit! And if you think I'm going to stick around and put up with it? You've got another thing coming."

He could hear her crying. Her voice was coming from deep inside the room. Probably the en-suite.

"Cat—"

"—Leave me alone! Go! Just… leave me alone!" She was crying.

Jarod stood up unsteadily. There was no point. Not tonight. Not in the state she was in. He knew he hadn't done anything wrong—his rational mind told him. She'd understand in the morning, when she will have had calmed down.

"Fuck it," he mumbled to himself. "What's the difference now? Might as well have another one."

He settled himself on the couch. He looked at the amber liquid, the glass twirling in his hand. He took a big gulp and felt the whiskey do its job. He closed his eyes. Everything was quiet now, like nothing had ever happened.

He took another swig. The glass was empty now. He got up. Screw the glass. He took the bottle back.

This time he drank straight from the bottle. He felt his body sink like a ship to the depth of the ocean. He coughed. He could hear someone weeping in the distance. The sob was coming from far, far away—almost like a dream.

"Cat—" he garbled.

Then he passed out.

****

Jarod jumped.

Something had woken him up.

His head felt like it was going to explode. It wasn't the shimmer this time, it was definitely the heavy booze from the previous night. It had been a long time since he had drunk that much.

He thought of going to Catalina, but thinking was as far as he got. He couldn't even open his eyes. They felt like there were a couple of sinkers holding them down and he depicted his eyelids being fishing lines. He imagined trying to reel in the fish—must be a whale at least— and his eyelids straining against the load.

Damn! He shouldn't have drunk so much. He used to enjoy going out on Friday nights and getting smashed with his buddies. But that had been a long time ago. and now his body did not welcome the abuse.

His thoughts veered to Catalina. There was not a sound. Did she stop crying and finally found comfort in sleep? He felt guilty. Women tended to do that to you. Whether it was your fault or not, it didn't make any difference. You were still guilty until proven innocent. But somehow you always felt bad. That's what really sucked.

Finally his eyes were opened.

It was still dark but daylight would soon appear. The room had that spectral glow you got when the sun was creeping up on a new day. It must have been 5:30'ish or close to 6am.

"Maybe I should go and see if she is okay," he said to himself, slowly coming out of his reverie.

I'll just go in and slowly slide into the sheets. Hopefully things will be better when she wakes up and she'll finally believe me.

He turned his head towards the bedroom. There was no light showing, meaning that she has probably gone back to sleep. He put one foot on the ground—it felt like lead. He tried to get up from the couch on which he had unceremoniously crashed.

He could feel every bone in his body as if he had just been involved in a major car accident and had gone through the windscreen. He guessed the narrow, hard couch was not welcomed by his body anymore than the booze, and it made sure that Jarod knew about it.

Don't abuse me like that you drunkard piss-a-shit, it seemed to be saying. *I'm gonna make sure you hurt and you'll think twice about putting me through this shit again.*

"Shut the fuck up," Jarod said to his unwilling limbs. "Just bear with me, okay? Just get me to my proper bed, and you can thank me later."

With a grunt Jarod managed to sit up and get his other leg on the ground. He looked at the bedroom door—it seemed a marathon away.

He got up a bit too quickly and felt the whole room spinning. This wasn't good. He sat right back down and closed his eyes. Slowly the spinning stopped.

He reopened his heavy eyelids and decided to make it to the bedroom on his hands and knees—that would be a safer approach. He let his body drop to the ground like a boneless chicken and pushed himself up on knees and elbows, and like a wavering buck that's been shot, he slowly made his way to the bedroom.

He got to the bedroom door and saw that it was slightly ajar. That's funny, he was sure that she had locked it the night before. Maybe she had changed her mind?

He pushed it open with his head and like a feline eyeing its prey—right, a feline with half-gallon of piss in him—he sluggishly made his way to the end of the bed. He raised his head above the back panel and peered at the landscape of sheets. Something was wrong. The terrain seemed too flat. If Catalina had been in there, he should have at least seen a mound. She wasn't really a big girl, but not exactly two-dimensional either.

He managed to get a little higher up and even-though the room was quite dark, he could distinguish a white, flat, thin square sitting on her pillow—a note. He felt bile rising up and tickling the base of his throat. This couldn't be good.

95

He rolled himself onto the bed and crawled to the piece of paper. He grabbed it and brought it close to his face.

As if on cue, the sun rose another degree above the horizon and the light now streaming in through the gap in the shades found its way, like a finger, to the paper that was displaying Catalina's hand writing.

Shit, even God's got his finger in the pie now."

He read the note:

Jarod,

I don't think I can do this anymore. In fact, I know I can't. I don't think that you are being faithful. I'm not stupid and I know what's going on. I don't know what you want from this relationship and now I can't say that I do either.

You always go out on weekends and tell me that you are meeting some kid out of the goodness of your own heart. Your shimmer, or whatever you want to call it, is making you unstable. It's scary and you should really see a head shrink.

I need a break. Maybe we both do.

Get your shit together and when you do, then maybe, just maybe... we'll see.

Cat.

Jarod let the letter drop from his hand. A cloud passed in front of the sun and the room was dark again. "Last ray of hope," he mumbled. "Even He is against me now."

He let his body collapse into the crumbled sheets, his face pushed against her pillow. He could smell her, almost as if she were still lying there—right next to him.

But she wasn't. He was all alone. Well not entirely. The shimmer could always be counted on to show its ugly face.

The *fucking* shimmer.

CHAPTER 13

"You think so?" Jarod said and took another drag from his cigarette.

"Dude," James said, "I don't know, I mean, that's what I heard anyway."

James took a drag himself. He looked worried. "Well, from what I heard, she spent a couple of hours at HR, and I don't think they were having a picnic there."

Jarod's lips formed thin line. "Then what?"

"When she came back, she had that stupid smirk on her face. You know, like she just won the lottery and doesn't wanna show it. Anyway dude, I think it's not looking good. You'd better watch your steps from now on. This is serious shit."

A man in a suit walked passed. James lowered his voice. "Dude, you gonna lose your job if you are not careful."

"Mate," Jarod said and inhaled one last puff before throwing his consumed butt into a puddle. "At this stage, I don't really give a shit."

James frowned. "What do you mean you don't give a shit? This is your job we are taking about. The market is really crap out there. Finding another job will take ages."

"That's not the point. The point is that...Cat left me. So honestly, I don't give a fuck about anything right now."

"Why? You guys are so good together! Did you have an argument or something?"

James pulled out another cigarette and passed it to Jarod. Jarod took it gladly. Who gave a shit about lung cancer right now?

"Mate, I got drunk last night. Lost track of time and came home pretty late. She was waiting up."

"Oh, crap!"

Jarod sighed. "Yep, crap. To cut a long story short, she thinks I'm having an affair."

"Dude! Seriously?" His lips tightened and he looked at Jarod suspiciously. "You are not right? I mean...cheating on her?"

"What?" retorted Jarod. "Come on mate, you know me better than that. I love her! There's no way I would do something like that."

James raised his hands in surrender. "I know, I know, I'm sorry. I know you love her… just had to ask." He thought for a few second. "So what makes her think you're cheating on her?"

Jarod took a drag from his cigarette. "Well, you know, I came home late a few times, when I went to meet Mary."

"Mary?"

"Yeah, you know *Mary*! The kid I was telling you about. The one who can also see the shimmer. You know, the one that lives with her grandma."

James smacked his head, almost dropping his cigarette. "Oh right, okay, got it. Sorry, I remember now. Go on."

"Because of my little disappearances, and even though I told her the truth, she got it into her head I'm seeing someone else."

"Mmmm..." James said and flicked his second butt.

"Yes, mmmm....my thoughts exactly, mate. We had an argument last night, or should I say this morning, and she locked herself in our bedroom. So, I decided to sleep on the couch with a couple of whiskeys, hoping that she would eventually calm down by the morning."

"Okay, and?"

"Well, I guess she didn't," he said removing the crumbled note she had left on the bed from his shirt pocket. He unfolded it and passed it on to James. "I woke up feeling like shit, managed to drag myself into the bedroom to smooth things out and, well instead of finding her in bed, I found this."

James took it and read it for what seemed like an eternity. Jarod could see a deep furrow forming between his eyes. The furrow got deeper and deeper as he got further into the letter. Once reaching the end, James looked up. "Shit dude," he finally said. "This is not good."

"No shit, Sherlock," Jarod said and dropped his butt into the puddle near his feet, his ears automatically catching the familiar hiss. He always wanted to make sure that his fags were properly put out. Causing a fire for something so stupid was the last thing he wanted to do, although smoking in a garage full of cars wasn't exactly smart.

James looked increasingly worried. "So what you gonna do, dude?"

Jarod was staring into emptiness, his eyes unfocused. "I don't know mate. I really don't know. What should I do? What *can* I do? Should I try to find out where she is staying and talk to her maybe?"

James considered for a few seconds. "Nah," he said, "I think it's better to let her be for a couple of days. She will start to miss you and realized that she may have jumped the gun."

"You think so?" Jarod moved aside as a Tesla decided to park right where he was standing.

Just to piss me off!

He peered through the windscreen to see who the fuck would choose this particular spot when there were hundreds of others.

His jaw tightened. "Fuck!" he muttered though clenched teeth, just enough for James to hear him. "You've gotta be kidding me." Out of all the spaces in the car-park, the bitch had to choose that one.

James glanced through the windscreen of the Tesla. It was Margaret. "She definitely did it on purpose the bitch," he whispered to Jarod as she opened the door and stumbled out like a polar-bear leaving the confines of its hibernating pit.

She walked passed them, not even bothering to look at Jarod. But then she stopped and turned to James.

"Hello James," she smiled, but to Jarod it looked more like a smart-arse smirk.

"Hi Margaret," James said, trying to sound normal.

"Enjoying your little break?" she asked sarcastically.

James was taken aback but pretended not to have noticed the sarcasm. "Well, yeah, gotta get away from that from that terminal once in a while. You know, bad for your eyes and all that."

Her back was deliberately tuned towards Jarod to make sure that he knew he didn't exist.

"I see," she said, her mouth twisting to one side. "Well plenty of work to be done I'm sure. Don't take too long now."

What the fuck? Seriously! Jarod couldn't believe her audacity. He couldn't hold it anymore. "Oh don't worry, *boss*," he hissed, making sure to emphasize the word boss. "We will be good little bunnies and go back to our burrows to slave away like the nice little employees we are."

James's eyes widened in surprise.

Jarod didn't care.

Margaret didn't even flinch at his remark. After a few seconds, she slowly turned around to finally acknowledge him. "Oh!" she lied, "I didn't see you there, Jarod."

"What? What do you mean you didn't see me there?" He blurted out. "You almost ran me over."

"Oh no... Mr. Johnson," she said in her sweetest voice. "If I had wanted to run you over, I would have. But don't you worry now, I will, one way or another...run you over; or should I say, run you *out*."

And without waiting for an reply, she walked off, leaving James and Jarod with their chins to the ground.

All Jarod could do was to whisper the only word that could find its way to his vocal chords. "Bitch!"

Just as the word came out, Margaret disappeared. Not through the door but from his vision—his right eye, to be more precise. The door itself was shimmering. Jarod put his head in both his hands. It felt like a volcano ready to erupt and his brain was going to explode. He put his hand on the hood of Margaret's car to support himself as his knees started to buckle underneath him. He felt himself go down.

He felt a strong hand grab him under his left armpit, preventing him from hitting the hard concrete floor head first. Maybe it would have been better to have let it happen, just to stop the excruciating pain that was developing.

"Dude? Dude! Are you okay?"

It was James' voice. He was sure James must have been loud but as the world around him was starting to dissipate, he could only distinguish it as if it were coming from a long way away, like at the end of a long tunnel. "I...mate...I," he mumbled, trying to form words that just wouldn't come out.

James cradled his head and lay it on the dirty garage floor. With his remaining good eye, Jarod saw him look around, panic in his eyes, but it seemed that there was only the two of them enjoying a health stick. He felt his cheeks been slapped. He wasn't sure how hard.

"Hey! You okay?" James's voice sounded more and more distant. Jarod's eyes were closed now but the shimmer was still here.

Then he saw it...

It was like looking through a dirty window filmed with oil. Through the smudges, he was able to discern legs—many legs, like people walking by and him sitting down on a curb.

He couldn't be dreaming for God's sake! He knew where he was—on the floor of a dirty car park! His eyes were closed but he knew he was awake. He could see them, however—the legs. They were there and they were real. Except for the greasy window, there were as solid as if he were sitting at a street corner.

Yet, there was no sound. The footsteps were like in a silent movie. Now he realized that there were no colors either. Everything was black and white.

The image started to waver. The shimmer was coming back.

"Dude?" This time, James' voice was louder. He could feel his hand cradling the back of his head. The headache was also gone, just as fast as it had appeared. The shimmer itself started to waver—if a shimmer could actually waver.

His eyes fluttered open. He could see James' face peering down at him. The deep lines that had formed on his forehead showed Jarod that he must have looked like shit.

James pulled his head up and rested it on his thigh. "Dude?" This time he could hear him clearly. "You're back! Hey, are you okay? You scared me! Is it that shimmer thing again?"

"I...I..." His mouth felt like sand-paper. "I...yes, the shimmer," he managed to mumble. "It was the shimmer."

James blew out a long breath. "You okay now right? Do you want to go to hospital? You almost hit your head. This is really dangerous, you know? You should really see someone."

"No, please, no." This is the last thing Jarod wanted—to go and see another shrink. He was starting to come out of it anyway. Slowly but surely. "No, seriously, I'm okay now...but I saw it. I mean them."

"It? Them? What are you talking about?"

"The legs. The legs walking passed..."

James frowned "The *what?*"

Jarod closed his eyes and tried to remember. "The legs....I saw them. They were real mate, they were there. I saw them..."

CHAPTER 14

Somehow, back at his desk, Jarod was staring at his blank terminal. He didn't have the energy to turn it on. He was thinking of what had just happened in the parking lot. He had definitely seen legs walking past, and he definitely had not been dreaming.

Was Dr. Andrews right? Did he actually just see an other side? A parallel universe? Were those the legs of people going on their daily errands in a parallel universe? Leaving their lives simultaneously? Could there actually be more than one? And why not?

But why me? What is so special about me? What have I done to deserve this?

The phone on his desk rang.

The last thing he wanted to do right now was to talk to someone. But Jarod picked up the phone anyway and put the earpiece to his ear.

"Hello?" he said.

"Hello, yes, is this Jarod Johnson?"

Jarod didn't recognize the voice. He frowned. "Yes, this is him. Who am' I talking to?"

"Jarod, this is Fern Lay from Human Resource." It was a woman's voice.

Oh shit, here we go!

"Okay...and?" he said, knowing very well what this was all about.

There was a moment's hesitation before she spoke. "Well, Jarod, the reason I'm calling is because we have received a couple of complaints about you, and I would just like to clear some things up and hear your side of he story."

Jarod closed his eyes. He had to make an excuse. He didn't want to deal with this right now. "Right...but..."

The voice cut off his thoughts. "Would you be free to come down to the 6th floor right now?"

"Well, I'm a bit busy but I guess I can if it's important," he said reluctantly.

"Okay, that's great Jarod. When you get down to reception, just ask for Fern and someone will show you in. Ill see you soon."

She hung up before he had time to confirm.

****

Fern was an elegant woman. Jarod could see that she was the kind of woman who took time everyday to take care of how she looked. He noticed the ring on her finger, which told him she was most likely married. On her desk was a silver picture frame in which sat a photograph of two teenagers in a park. "Okay, have a seat, please," Fern said.

This was a career woman. A woman who juggled work and family and still managed to take care of herself. He didn't know how people like this could do it—find time for everything. Did they actually get any sleep at all?

"Right," she said and smiled at him as he finally settled in a chair facing her. The office itself was small but had a personal touch, as if to make her feel somewhat at home. Jarod thought that was probably because this was where she spent most of her time—sad.

Her smile was friendly and it made Jarod instantly feel more at ease.

This may not be so bad after all.

It didn't look like the smile of somebody who was about to put him in the street.

She opened a manila folder, and Jarod could see a couple of sheets with the bank's logo showing on the top right hand corner. He managed to see his name but wasn't able to discern anything that was written below it.

She looked up. "How are you Jarod? Everything okay?"

"Yes, I think so." Jarod hesitated, not really wanting to commit and lay out all his problems on the table.

"Okay, well that's good. I know you are busy, so I'm going to get straight to the point."

"Okay," Jarod said, knowing fairly well that it wasn't going to be okay.

Her smiled dropped and a concerned furrow appeared between her eyes. "Jarod, we have received some complaints about your performance lately. And actually, more than once."

"Well, yeah," Jarod said leaning back on his chair and crossing his arms defensively. "And let me guess. This is from Margaret Wong, right?"

"I'm sorry, but I'm not allowed to disclose the source. All HR matters are confidential. All I can say for now is that there have been several complaints in regards to both your performance and your behavior in the office."

Jarod knew where this was going. He could feel the anger growing inside him like a hot furnace.

"Listen," he said. "*This* is honestly not my fault and she had it coming. She's had it for me since day one for no reason. Just check my appraisal and you won't find a single positive comment coming from her."

How dare the bitch actually go ahead and complain to HR? Couldn't she handle her own shit? He saw Fern analyzing him. He could see in her eyes that she understood him—maybe she also had a bitch boss.

She nodded, as if she understood. "Listen, work is not a personal vendetta, and you cannot go around calling your boss names, no matter how you feel about her and how angry you are. This is what Human Resources is for. If you have a problem in or out of the office, then you can come and talk to us."

"Okay but..." Jarod said trying to come up with another, more convincing excuse.

Fern leaned forward, but this time, the sympathy had gone out of her eyes. So much for that. Her voice came out harsher. "No buts. Please, Jarod, it wasn't just this incident. There has also been, on another two occasions, complaints about your performance. Deadlines missed and projects being delayed. You have also been seen living work before 5:30 and not coming back."

"Yes, that happened a couple of times and I'm sorry," he said. "But I had a major headache, it wasn't my fault."

Shit, this wasn't going well. The bitch had really gone for the kill. It was time for some honesty. "You see," he continued. "I've been having these really bad headaches and when they start, it's impossible for me to work anymore. It's just killing me. It's been getting worse and worse and I know it's affecting my work. In fact, not just my work but also my whole life."

Fern leaned back. A look of concern crossed her face. "Have you been to see a doctor?" she asked. "If you are having these headaches, you do know that you have medical coverage and you can see a doctor right?"

"Yes, I know." replied Jarod. "In fact, I have already been to the doctor, but they don't have any idea what's going on.

They think I'm going crazy and having hallucinations. But I know how I feel and what I see."

A crease formed on Fern's perfectly made-up face. "What do you mean, you know what you see?"

"The legs, the people," he said without thinking. "It's the shimmer, the parallel universe."

Her face froze. "What are you talking about Jarod? Parallel universe? Legs?"

Jarod realized he had said too much and must have sounded like a total lunatic. From the look on her face, that's exactly how he seemed to appear to her.

"Jarod," she said, confirming his thoughts and forcing him to come back down to earth. "I think you need some time off."

"But—" Jarod said, not believing what he had just heard.

"I think you need some time off work to try and sort out whatever is happening. We have physiologists whom we can recommend, and you will be fully reimbursed by the bank. Whatever it is, the headaches, the...parallel universe, you need to see someone."

Jarod didn't like where this was going. "I'm not crazy!" he shouted.

Fern didn't flinch.

He went on, "What I'm telling you is real." He knew how crazy he must have sounded. He leaned forward on his chair.

Fern recoiled. There was fear in her eyes. After a moment of silence, she regained her composure. "Jarod, I'm *not* saying you are crazy. It is obvious, however, that something is wrong and you need to see someone to find out what it is. What's more, whatever it is, it's affecting your work and your attitude towards your team members. Therefore, we have to fix this and you really need some time off." She leaned forward, making her point clear. "I'm going to recommend a month off, and I'm going to give you a list of doctors we work with. After that, whatever the problem is, it will hopefully be fixed and you will be able to go back to work."

Jarod was flabbergasted. "A month off? Seriously?" That's all he needed right now. She thought he was a lunatic. Shit! They were really doing this. The bitch had won.

Fern stared at him.

Jarod had to try to find a way for him to stay in his job. Surely he couldn't be so indispensable. They needed him. "What about the two projects I am working on?"

"Don't you worry about that for now. They are not your problem anymore. They will be taken care of, I'm sure. And since they have already been delayed, it won't be much of an issue."

"What about my pay? I can't afford a month without my pay."

"You will be on half pay for that month."

"Half pay? What? I have bills to pay! I can't live on half pay!"

Fern seemed to be losing her patience. She didn't look so friendly anymore. She leaned forward again and her eyes held his stare. "Mr. Johnson, listen to me and understand this. I'm trying to do the best I can for you under the circumstances. In fact, I'm doing you a favor so you don't have to lose your job after what happened. I'm not sure why you acted the way you did but I'm sure that you must have had your reasons... whatever they may be. Let's just say that your continuation in missing deadlines and the fact that you have directly insulted your direct line manager are not things that we take lightly. So please, bear with me and understand that this is the best I can do under the current circumstances."

Jarod sat back, a defeated look on his face. Maybe she was right. Maybe he did need some time off to sort out his shit. And honestly, it wasn't like he was going to starve at half pay anyway. He looked up. Fern's expression had softened. Maybe she really was giving him a break. He should try to put himself in her shoes. She was just doing her job and he was being an ass.

He sat back. "Okay…I'm sorry," he said. "Let's go with what you said. You are right. I think it will be good for me to take a month off and sort myself out. I really do need a break."

"I'm glad you understand," she said looking relieved. "You can go back to your desk and pack whatever you need. Then you can come back here and we will fill a leave of absence form."

Jarod stood up and extended his hand. Fern took it awkwardly. She didn't seem to expect the gesture.

"Thanks for your help," he said and squeezed her hand gently. "Believe it or not, I do understand you are trying to help me, and I appreciate it."

Before she could reply, he let go of her hand, turned around and stepped out.

Once reaching his desk, he felt like he should at least tell James, but he was nowhere to be found—probably in another meeting. He'd call him later.

He picked up his bag and headed towards the exit. Just as he was reaching the pantry, he felt a gaze, like something burning a hole at the back of his head. He turned around and there she was—the bitch—with a smile on her face.

He stopped and gave her a hard look but her sarcastic sneer didn't waver. In fact, it seemed to have widened. He wanted so much to say something—to give her the finger. But the better side of him told him not to give her the satisfaction. Instead he smiled and winked. Her smirk disappeared.

He turned on his heels and stepped out of this office, feeling that at least he had won a battle.

A very tiny battle.

CHAPTER 15

Jarod opened the door to his apartment. It felt so empty. Just the thought that Catalina wasn't going to walk through the front door after her day at the office was depressing. Nothing to look forward to. All the efforts they had made to build up this relationship had all been in vain.

When he had met her, she was a bit of a party animal. The kind of girl who looked liked she wouldn't be ready to settle down any time soon. A bit like her friend Sophie. But he had changed that in her. He had tamed her to enjoy coming to a place you could call home and enjoy each-others' company—of not needing anyone else.

Jarod dropped his bag next to the entrance, not even bothering to take his shoes off—something Catalina was adamant about. He headed straight for the kitchen instead, straight for the inevitable.

"Fuck it," he muttered to himself. "It's not like she's coming back anyway."

With the bottle of whiskey in hand, not bothering with a glass, he walked back to the lounge room and settled himself on his favorite couch. Well at least his couch and whiskey didn't quit on him.

He opened the cap slowly. His mind knew drinking was wrong, yet so right. He drank increasingly lately and didn't like what he was becoming—an alcoholic? No, maybe not. Not yet anyway.

Alcoholics can't live without their daily fuel. For Jarod, he believed it was just a phase—like just to settle his mind. To take the edge off, sort of speak. But wasn't that how alcoholism started in the first place? A reason to forget? A reason to feel a sense of release? To put things into perspective?

He knew he was trying to make excuses for himself and for one of his too-many night caps.

He let the cap drop to the floor, next to the couch, and brought the bottle his lips. The Johnny Walker descended slowly. He felt the slow burn and didn't tip the bottle back up until the heat had settled at the pit of his stomach.

As he looked up, he got a descent head spin. The TV set was going one way, then the other. "Wow." he bawled, breaking the stillness around him. "Take it easy, young fella! It's not like you in a hurry, now it is."

His own voice sounded way too loud in the stillness surrounding him, but he needed to break the silence, even at the expense of feeling like a moron.

The heavy dose of alcohol made him feel worse. He had all the time in the world. All the time to get smashed and nobody would give two shits if he were to be found drowned in his own puke. Maybe it would be better this way. He would do himself and everyone else a favor.

He brought the bottle back to his lips and took another swig. Again he didn't bring the bottle back down until the whiskey hit his guts. His head was spinning nicely now. The lounge room seemed to be going round in circles as if he were sitting at the center of a merry-go-round.

Without thinking, and as if having switched to auto-mode, his free hand reached deep into his pants pocket and he pulled out his cell phone. He clicked the auto-dial button number one and heard the connecting sound followed by the familiar ringing tone of Catalina's cell phone.

The phone kept ringing but Jarod didn't hang up. He wanted to hear her voice. He let it go to voice-mail. He knew somehow, even in his fucked-up state, that she wouldn't pickup.

He waited for the beep and tried to sound sober. "Err, hi..." he slurred, not really knowing what he wanted to say. "It's... it's me, Jarod. Do you mind, if you got time, of course... like... give me a call back? Ya know, when ya free? If...if it's... you know...not too much trouble?"

That sounded pathetic and he knew it. She was probably right there, by the phone, and had all the time in the world. "I' like t' talk to ya. I...well, I luv ya. I luv ya and I mis' ya. M' sorry 'bout everyt' ing. Can we..."

"Beeeeeep!" The recorder had run out of time.

Jarod let the phone drop. He could feel a tear rolling down his right cheek. It reached the corner of his lips. He opened them slightly and tasted the salt. He felt another tear. This time running down his left cheek. This one didn't reach the corner of his lips but rolled right down to his chin, pooling up and eventually cascading into a tiny puddle, leaving a round little wet patch on his shirt.

More tears started to flow. This time he couldn't hold them anymore. His right hand, still holding the bottle, managed to lower the offending amber liquid on the floor without spilling a drop.

His shoulders shook uncontrollably as a fresh flood of tears streamed down his face. The sobbing followed. First just a whimper and then a guttural sound escaping his gaping mouth. His body was shaking uncontrollably. His shoulders and neck forming tight cords as the muscles tightened to alleviate the frantic grip of despair swallowing him.

As if listening from deep within, he heard a roar come out like the rage he had been holding back. The scream was so loud that he had a second to wonder if it would rip his throat out. Spittle flew from his gaping jaw. His eyes two narrow slits. His nostrils flared and his face turned red from the blood rushing through his stretched-out veins into his brain.

He could smell himself now. The mixture of sweat and whiskey oozing from every pore. A smell of rot coming from deep within. A smell of annihilation, fear and desperation. The mingled stench of an animal trapped in a cage with no way out, like a lamb on its way to the slaughter house.

His hands flew in all directions as if trying to battle the phantoms surrounding his despair. He screamed and screamed and screamed even more until his larynx gave up the attempt to let his sorrow escape in a hemorrhage of froth and howling. The crescendo reached its climax and then his depleted body surrendered.

He could only hear the sobbing now. Like a raging river reaching the end of its rapids and finding tranquil water to settle upon. He felt his shoulders relax and the heaviness of his wasted, exhausted soul. He couldn't even lift a finger any longer, like all the weight of the world had settled upon his shoulders.

Everything was black. There were no colors anymore. He had descended down to the abyss. The sounds... the smells... even his vision—black.

His body, as limp as a dishrag, toppled forward. His legs failing underneath him. He felt himself—his limbs in disarray —hit the floor hard. But inside—he felt nothing.

He was numb. His body had barely resolved itself to its dismembered position when his brain also gave up. His eyelids finally closed, surrendering to the dark.

The emptiness.

The void.

****

A ring.

Jarod's hand felt numb as he blindly tried to pick up his cell phone. Like a spider homing on its prey, his fingers finally reached the receiver.

The ringing continued.

Jarod managed to wrap a couple of fingers around the phone. Luckily, the cell had fallen next to the couch. In one movement, ignoring the ants biting every inch of the arm he had fallen asleep on, he brought it to his ear.

"Hewwo…" he said through a tongue that seemed to fill his entire mouth, forcing him to speak through whatever gap he could find.

A woman's voice came through the receiver. "Hello? Jarod? Is that you?" To his disappointment, it wasn't Catalina.

"Mmmmm… yeaaaah Whozzzz dat." Damn whiskey Why did you always have to feel like shit afterwards—no ifs or buts.

"Jarod. This is Sophie. Catalina's friend. You remember me?"

Yes he did. He sure did. And he was pretty sure that she was one of the reasons why Catalina had left him. God only knew what she had put into her head to make her think that he was seeing someone else.

"Yeah, I remember," he slurred, one eye finally opened.

He heard a sigh. "Jarod? Are you drunk?"

"Me? Nahhhhhh. Imma z sober az imma ever gonna beee." What the hell was wrong with him? His mouth felt like he was chewing on a whole wad of cotton. His other eye was now opened. The room was spinning like a mother-fucker and the light penetrating his pupil felt like a sharp knife being driven into his head.

He heard the phone being put down at the other end and Sophie was whispering to someone close to her. "Ellooo?! I can hear youuu! P...put Ca-alina on willyaaaa? I...I know shezzz here!"

The other side made a clumping noise then the phone was picked up once more. "Jarod. This is Sophie again. Catalina is with me. It's obvious that you are totally out of it and so now is not a good time. She'll call you back later."

"Noooooo." Jarod said desperately. "Noooo! I wan' talk to'er now!"

Sophie's voice rose. "Jarod! You listen to me! You fucked up and Catalina is my friend. She is staying with me right now, and if you want to see her again then you'll need to get your shit together."

Jarod didn't have the energy to argue. Begging was easier. "P...pleazzzzeeeeee…" was all he could manage.

"Jarod, no!" she said. "Catalina is my friend and I will not let her go through this shit. Not if I can help it. She loved you and trusted you and she had been through enough already."

"But...I...I gign't goo a'ythin! I thwearrr..."

This time, the only response was a click at the other end. Sophie had hung up on him.

He let the cell drop next to the couch, not even bothering to hang-up the call. The room was still spinning badly so he closed he eyes—the spinning didn't stop.

There was no sound coming from the streets. It must have been late at night or early morning. He didn't have the energy to look at his watch—that would have meant opening he eyes. The lingering odor of whiskey was pretty bad. It seemed to have impregnated everything around him. His sweat, added to the stench, made it almost unbearable to take a breath without feeling the bile piling up at the back of his throat. He felt the rancid taste of regurgitated whiskey in his mouth. He swallowed it back with a grimace.

He could feel his body sinking into the carpet as if it were made of quicksand. Why did she have to call back if she wasn't going to talk to him? To make him feel worse? To show him that she wasn't coming back to him? And that Sophie bitch was probably making it worse by telling her that he was drunk. Why did she have to call back when he was so fucked up and slurring like a fucking retard?

No job. No cat. No...nothing.

His hand dropped. Limp. His fingers brushed the neck of the bottle—amazing, it was still standing—the whiskey intact inside.

He tried to pick it up for another swig. The bottle felt so heavy, like that thirty pound weight he still couldn't curl. His fingers gave up the herculean attempt at lifting the bottle to his alcohol-stricken lips, and it ended up on its side, its final contents being sucked into the carpet.

Deeper and deeper he sank into the abyss of despair—drowning in a sea of grief. He would die like this. And why not? Asphyxiated in his own puke.

His feet wanted to feel something solid but he sank deeper and deeper into the bottomless pit of his own agony.

Finally, to his solace, Jarod passed out for the second time.

CHAPTER 16

Jarod looked up. The building still looked the same. Old and black with grime lining the walls that had never seen a brush or a coat of paint since they had been erected. The building looked like it shouldn't exist.

Yet, he knew that to some, and that included Pawpaw and Mary, it was what they had to call home. Living in misery and poverty and working to the bone just to make ends meet. But for what? Just to live a life? To survive? To subsist? Was that what it was all about? Not being able to leave a mark? To at least be remembered? How could they find any happiness with such an existence? How could they carry on? Survival was the game.

Jarod had read somewhere that only ten percent of the world's population lives a somewhat comfortable life. This figure seemed mind boggling to him. As far as these ten percent were concerned, it seemed like everybody else lived the way they did. Yet, it was far from being the case.

As he approached the entrance, the first thing that hit him face on was the lingering smell of urine. Did all common decency vanish when poverty set in? Jarod couldn't understand how anyone could live in these conditions, but at the same time, he knew that it was easy to judge when you were standing on the other side of the fence.

After having made his way up the dark uninviting putrid stairs, he ultimately reached Mary's outer steel gate. Why couldn't they at least install a doorbell so that you didn't have to call the person you were visiting just to get them to open the gate? He reluctantly but obligingly called Mary's cell phone and waited patiently for her to pick up in the hope that she wouldn't take so long so as to find him lying in the pool of filth that was surrounding him, overcome by the stench.

He could hear the ring-tone coming from his earpiece as well as its echo emanating from Mary's habitat. Somehow the word apartment didn't seem to quite fit.

"Waiiii." Mary answered in her tiny nasal voice.

Jarod was relieved. "Mary! It's Jarod! How are you? I'm standing at your outer gate. Could you please come out and open it for me?"

The door behind Jarod opened a fraction and behind its frame he saw a single wrinkled eye peering at him through matted gray hair, probably wondering what the hell a foreigner was doing in this building. Jarod attempted a smile but the door was quickly slammed and the wrinkled inquisitive eye disappeared as quickly as it had materialized.

Still figuring out what had just happened, Mary's voice brought him out of his stupor. "Ahhh! Jarod! Me come now. You wait ,okay?"

"Okay Mary, I'll wait," Jarod said thinking that a minute more of this reek would mean the redecoration of Mary's bathroom. After a few seconds, he finally heard Mary's creaking inner door and the footsteps that followed. Her face appeared behind the steel door, and it reminded Jarod of looking at someone behind prison bars. Well, maybe even a prison would probably have been in better condition.

Her face was all smile. If a grin could have looked any bigger, thought Jarod, you would have been able to fit a Big

Mac without even touching the sides. It warmed his heart and the smell and filth were instantly forgotten. The clang of the latch released the locking mechanism and as the gate was pushed open, it's hinges cried out in a desperate call for WD40. Jarod had to remember to bring a can next time.

With a hand to his nose, he followed Mary down the narrow passage whilst avoiding the permanent yellow paddle that sat halfway between the gate and her inner door.

Having entered Mary's apartment, he found the empty cane chair and settled into it, his legs silently thanking him for the respite. He looked up and realized Mary's smile had vanished and was replaced by a frown on her skinny young face.

"Mary?" he said. "Are you okay? You look worried."

"Oh, yes, Jarod, me okay now," she said and stepped into the kitchen-bathroom to retrieve two cups and a jug of water. "You like water with lemon, Jarod? Pawpaw make it. Is very nice and cold."

"Yes, that would be nice," Jarod said, welcoming the idea of the smell of lemon while taking the cups from Mary and pouring them both a glass-full of the homemade lemonade.

He took a sip and it tasted good.

"Mary," he said. "Are you sure you're okay?"

Mary looked down at her hands. "Me not know. Me see many time, what you call..." she looked up inquiring.

"The shimmer?"

"Yes! Yes, the shimmer. Me see many time. And me head very hurt."

Jarod leaned forward and put his glass on the table, keeping his eyes locked on Mary's anxious face. "You did? What do you mean many times? How many times Mary?"

This was a worry. It seemed as if Mary may have had it worse than him.

"Many time," she said and placed her own glass on the table. She looked down as if reliving a painful memory. "Too

120

many time me see shimmer. And many time me head feel so hurt."

Jarod frowned. "Mary, when you say many times, you mean like once a week? Or like everyday? What do you mean?"

Mary looked up at Jarod. Her face was young, but Jarod could tell her eyes had seen more than they should have. "Sometime each day. Me see shimmer today and day before and also three day before."

Holy shit! This is much worse than me.

He placed his hand on top of hers. "Mary, was it just the shimmer or did you actually see something else? Like legs? Or people maybe?"

Mary didn't remove her hand and in fact seemed to welcome Jarod's caring touch. "Yes, me saw persons. Many persons walk pass. But like window on front. Hard to see persons. And then go away."

His hand involuntary squeezed Mary's own. "Wow! That's amazing! We saw the same thing Mary! You and I actually saw the same thing."

Mary's mouth formed an 'O' and her eyes opened widely. "You see also, Jarod?"

A huge smile broke on Jarod's face. He couldn't hide his excitement. "Yes! Yes! I saw it too! The legs, I saw the legs also! It was like I was lower, like maybe sitting down or something. And. the legs were going passed, like people were in the street, maybe on their way to work or something."

This was amazing! This was really amazing! And it also proved that it wasn't just a hallucination! This proved that it was real and that he was not the only one. Somehow both Mary and him were seeing the very same thing.

Could this be a window to a parallel universe? Could this actually be what Dr. Andrews was talking about? Was it possible that both Mary and him could see what no one else could? Or maybe not no one actually. Were there other people around that were currently experiencing the same thing?

There seemed to be more questions than answers, but at least for now, Jarod knew that he wasn't the only one and that he certainly wasn't crazy.

Jarod came back from his own thoughts. "You know what I think is happening?" he said excitedly.

A worried line appeared on Mary's brow. "No, me not know. Me want know. Me think me crazy and head hurt very hurt. Me really scare."

Jarod, still holding her hand, gazed into her eyes. He could see her fear. There was no doubt that they were sharing something more than just friendship. He tried to reassure her. "Don't be scared. You and I have a special gift. I think we are able to see into another universe—another *world* Mary."

Mary looked lost. "Other what?"

This was going be a hard to explain. "Let me try to explain in simple terms."

"Okay," Mary said. She pinched her lips and narrowed her eyes in concentration.

"Do you know what a universe is?"

"Yes, me know. It stars and sun."

"Yes, Mary, that's it, stars and sun." He was relieved that at least he didn't have to explain what the universe was.

He said. "Do you know what a multi-universe is?"

"No, sorry Jarod, me not know what is multi-universe."

"Okay, let me explain. Don't worry ,okay? One step at a time."

"Okay," Mary said. She seemed entranced, her eyes did not leave Jarod while her hand reached blindly for her glass of lemonade.

Jarod took a sip of his own lemonade and continued. "Well, the word multi actually means many. So many universes ,okay?"

Mary's fingers finally managed to find the glass and without even a glance, she brought to her lips. She took a sip. "Okay, many universe, okay."

"Good! Now step two," continued Jarod patiently. "So you know that we, you and I and all the people that we see are in one universe, correct?"

"Yes, one universe, me know. Only one universe."

"Right, well Mary, let me tell you something." Jarod leaned forward to make sure that he had her full attention. "In fact, there may be more than one universe. There may be many, many..."

Mary looked bewildered. Her head jerked back as if to avoid a sudden blow. "I...I sorry Jarod, I not understand. How can many universes?"

Jarod's mouth twisted to one side. "Well, I think so anyway. There is a theory that there may be." He took another sip, not really tasting the lemonade. His mind was too preoccupied. This could take a while.

"Listen," he continued. "Whether there is or not, we don't really know. Well, not one hundred percent anyway. That's why it's called a theory, cause we are not sure. Just imagine for now that there are many universes ,okay?"

"Okay," replied Mary taking a large swallow of the lemonade herself.

Jarod nodded. "Good. So what I really want to say is that you and I are special."

"Special? You and me? But why?"

"We are special, my friend, because it looks like you and I are able to see into one of these universes," he replied and wondered how she would take it, or even if it made any sense to her.

"You say..." Mary said placing her glass back down on the table and making sure that her shaky hands wouldn't drop it, "that we see other universe? Like people not from here?"

"Yes!" Jarod said. He was relieved Mary was finally able to understand what he was trying to tell her. His shifted on his chair and leaned closer to her than he already was. He wanted to make sure that Mary wouldn't miss anything that he had to say.

"You see," he said, "you and I can see people that are like...like me and you. They have their own life, just like us and they don't know that we exist. They also believe that there is only one universe, just like we do." He took a deep breath and swallowed the remainder of his lemonade. He exhaled. "Do you understand what I'm saying?"

Mary's expression seemed to connect the dots. "Yes, me think me understand Jarod. Just me not understand why."

Jarod scratched his chin. "Why?" he asked, more to himself than to Mary. "Why indeed.." He turned back to her. "Mary. Listen, I don't know why this is happening, but it seems that you and I can see more and more. I wonder how far it will go and how much we will eventually see. I really hope that this is not for the rest of our life. If it is, I think that I'm gonna end up going crazy. I can't imagine this going on forever. I also can't imagine that there isn't a reason for it. There has to be. I mean, everything happens for a reason right?"

Jarod was talking more to himself now—he didn't expect an answer.

Mary was silent. She was looking at her hands as if trying to find an answer in the lines that's were crisscrossing her palms.

Jarod could see in her young face that she looked lost. She didn't deserve any of this. Why her? Wasn't her life difficult enough already without this shit? Poor kid. It was bad enough that he had to put up with it, but he could imagine Mary, cocooned in this fifteen-by-fifteen room, with an already hard enough life and now this crap. He was complaining, but it would be much worse for her, not to mentioned how scared she must feel.

At least, in a selfish way, Jarod felt a bit better that he wasn't the only one. If anything, it proved that he wasn't going crazy and that this — whatever it was—was real.

He went to grab another mouthful of his lemonade but realized that his glass was empty. Looking at his watch, he saw that it was almost six. "What time does Pawpaw come back Mary?".

Mary's head jerked up as if she had been in a trance. "Errr?" she mumbled, coming out of her reverie, her eyes meeting Jarod's own.

"I was asking what time Pawpaw will be back?"

Mary unglued her eyes from Jarod's and looked up at the clock on the opposite wall. The clock seemed huge in the confines of her tiny home—it showed 18.01. "Pawpaw here soon. She come six o'clock," she replied.

Jarod thought for a few seconds, his eyes quickly scanning the room. It was small, damp, dark...depressing. His heart sank. "Tell you what. How about I invite you and Pawpaw for diner. What do you say? I think we both need to clear our minds and some cheering up."

Mary's face lit up. "Diner?" she asked, surprised. "With me and Pawpaw?"

"Sure! Why not? I think I need this as much as you do. I don't think I really want to have dinner alone right now."

Mary's beautiful smile was back. It was as if everything had already been forgotten. Jarod wished it could be that easy for him also. Maybe it was easier when you were a kid—when your mind could accept anything.

She opened her mouth, but before a word came out, the rusty sound of the outer gate made its way to their ears. They heard the footsteps and the key to the inner door. The door opened revealing Pawpaw's wrinkled face.

She looked old and worn-out to Jarod, but the cracked smile that appeared at seeing him, showing the many gaps behind her corrugated lips told him there was nothing that he wanted more right now than to share a meal with the two people he cared the most about in the world right now.

CHAPTER 17

It was 2 o'clock in the morning when Jarod finally stood at his front door.

As he fumbled for his keys, he vaguely remembered the nice dinner with Mary and Pawpaw. Had it been? Chinese or Thai? Somehow the stop at the bar afterward and the numerous whiskeys had clouded his mind. After their diner, the thought of going back to his empty apartment hadn't seem very attractive—the stop-over at the bar had seemed like a better option. The intention was to have two quick shots and hit the road, but two had become three and somehow three—seven. Lucky the bar was at a walking distance.

He was pretty gone by now, but still, he didn't think he could sleep—not yet anyway.

Finally his fingers touched the key-ring, which happened to be an engraving of Catalina and him in better days. His thumb unconsciously rubbed the embossed design.

He brought the key-ring to his eye level and memories surged, memories he really didn't need right now. All he wanted was to forget, even if just for a little while.

After a few unsuccessful attempts, the key eventually found the key-hole.

Keys inserted into key-holes.

This triggered another memory he could have done without. A memory of Catalina lying there, naked. Her long limbs. One leg was always laying on his thigh when she fell into a deep slumber after a wonderful and exhausting session of the... key in the hole.

God he missed her...

Jarod entered his empty apartment and didn't even bother with the lights. The glow coming in from the street light facing his apartment was enough to give the lounge room an eerie luminescence from which Jarod's half closed eyes found comfort.

Somehow he made it into the kitchen. His right leg hit the low coffee table on his way there. But his leg was already as numb as an injected gum in a dentist's chair. The pain he should have felt was nothing more than a dull reminder that his leg was still attached to his body.

The whiskey bottle, although only half full, or half empty, whichever way you looked at it, was in its habitual place—top shelf, far enough not to be tempting but close enough to be grabbed at a moment's notice.

All too soon, Jarod was cocooned in his favorite chair, bottle in hand, ready to finish was he had already started. Who was counting anyway?

He took a swig and once again enjoyed the warmth of scotch settling where it belonged. The thought of Catalina, his job, his fucked-up life. He felt as desolated as raindrops on a grave.

Was that what the onset of depression was? He wasn't a sure but he knew right there and then that dying might be just the only answer right now. Not like anyone would miss him anyway. Good riddance to bad rubbish.

His head sank deeper and deeper into the cushion on which it was resting, and the angle was just right for his hand to bring the neck of the bottle into his gaping mouth. Most of the amber liquid, however, found its way down his shirt rather than the inlet to his parched throat.

But it didn't matter. Not anymore.

Jarod heard a car go past. Maybe it was Cat. Yeah, and maybe he was lying on a beach in Hawaii. He turned his head. Nothing to lose. It felt like a Boeing 747 taking a sudden sharp right to avoid a head on collision.

His head, half slumped on his shoulder, was now facing the front door. His mind was still conscious enough to conceptualize an image of Catalina walking through the door —anger in her eyes at seeing him in this state of drunkenness and desolation. But even a fight would have been a welcome respite—would have been better than the nothingness that appeared through the front door.

Suddenly he saw it. Hardly distinguishable at first but there nevertheless.

"Oh shit," he whimpered to himself "That's all I need."

A thought crossed his mind of swallowing a couple of aspirins in order to alleviate the inevitable headache that was bound to tag on. But he knew he was too fucked-up and wouldn't even be able to make it two steps from the couch without falling straight down on his face.

The door to his right started waving in and out and that's when he felt the sharp pain right behind his right eye. It felt like someone had suddenly jabbed it with a hot poker and was trying to pull his eyeball out. He screamed in pain and his hand shot up straight to his eye tried to cover it as if it would somehow relieve the agony. The pain was excruciating and like nothing he had ever felt before.

The shimmer was dancing crazily as if to mock him. He closed his eyes but nothing changed.

Jarod stumbled up with what sanity remained in his subconscious, telling him that he should be headed for the kitchen and make a cold compress, but before the thought even finished forming in his mind, he was already lying next to the couch, both hands grabbing his head in an attempt to squeeze out the throbbing torture. He had but a moment to think if it were possible at all for a head to explode from pain because, right now, he felt that there was no way it wasn't going to blow up and spread itself all over the walls.

Just before he passed out, his last mental picture was of the remains of his brain slowly drooling like slime and finding its way to the floor, forming a pool of sludge with little chips of bones resembling little white islands in a red sea of his last remaining thoughts.

CHAPTER 18

Jarod felt the warmth of the sun filtered through the bedroom window and onto his face. His eyes were still half-closed, and he was enjoying the few minutes between slumber and wake. His mind took time to wonder and recall the previous night's drinking session.

He turned to his right and tried to get into a more a comfortable position when he suddenly stopped and realized he would fall off the couch.

The couch didn't feel right, however. It felt softer. And wasn't that a pillow under his head? It certainly didn't feel hard like the couch's cushions.

Thoughts were sipping in slowly as his mind was trying to adjust to an awaken state. He remembered the dinner with Mary and Pawpaw and the one-too-many whiskeys that followed. He also remembered the half full bottle of whiskey.

The despair.

The solitude.

His eyes fluttered open and something was definitely wrong. Through the veil of his eyelashes, Jarod was not seeing what should have been—the apartment's entrance door— should he have been laying on the couch. Instead, he could see the lace curtain that was covering his bedroom window. Did he somehow make it back to bed last night? If he did, he certainly couldn't remember doing so.

He was pretty sure also that he had been wearing his clothes when he had passed out on the couch. Yet, here he was, not only in bed but also wearing his boxer shorts—not the ones he normally wore under his pants. but the ones he normally slept in.

He shook his head a couple of times. Normally, after a heavy night of drinking, it should have felt like his brain was inside a baby's rattle. But no. Nothing. His brain was in-cased squarely inside his cranium. There was no rattling and certainly no hangover. He knew for sure that he drank way too much last night and should have felt like rat shit this morning—but nothing, not even the slightest tinge of an onset of a headache.

That could be good... or bad. Could it mean that he was getting so used to drinking that his body didn't react anymore?

He sat up in bed and rubbed the remaining sleep from his eyes. He felt good. Actually, he felt too good. There were no aches and pains. His mind was clear and it made last night feel like a distant memory.

Jarod let his feet drop to the side of the bed and stood up. He expected to feel the usual wooziness that usually came after heavy drinking but even *that* was missing. He decided to go and have a shower, hoping the hot water might make him see things more clearly.

On his way to the bathroom, his eyes fell upon the couch from which he expected to see the remains of his bottle of whiskey.

But no.

Nothing.

The couch was in his habitual place. Not even an inch out of its usual position. And the whiskey bottle—no sign of it.

He must have done a lot more than he remembered last night. Seemed like he actually took the time to clean up, change into his pj's and make it to bed.

He lifted his right arm and brought his nose down to his armpit, expecting to just about pass out from the body odor that should have killed a skunk.

Again, nothing.

Or almost.

He could actually smell something. He took another whiff. Yep, there it was—Johnson's baby powder. No doubt about it.

Jarod had long ago switched to baby powder due to his allergy to deodorants. Catalina sometimes used to make fun of him when she lay her head on his chest and could smell him. She teased him that it was hard to imagine that such a stallion could smell like baby powder.

Jarod dropped his arm and decided to have a shower nonetheless. He needed to clear his head. Things didn't seem to be quite what they should have been this morning.

He took another two steps towards the bathroom and felt something soft under his foot. He looked down expecting to see his tee-shirt or maybe his boxers.

What he saw, however, made his head spin. He had to take a step backwards, his back finding the wall and his body sliding down until his buttocks touched the floor. His mind tried to make sense out of what he was seeing. He closed his eyes, trying to recall something, anything, that could rationalize the vision. But there was no recollection—nothing.

He reopened his eyes and slowly, his hand shaking, he reached for it. His fingers finally touching it. He could feel the soft silk caressing his skin. He picked it up and brought it close to his face. He put it against his face. He inhaled. He could smell it... he could smell *her*.

Catalina's panties were still warm.

He let his hand drop to his side with Catalina's sky blue panties still inside it—her smell still lingering around his flared

133

nostrils. He closed his eyes again. He tried to remember and again there wasn't even a hint as to what could have happened last night to explain anything that was happening now.

After a few seconds, Jarod snapped out of it.

"Okay," he rationalized to himself. "I woke up in bed instead of the couch. The whiskey bottle has disappeared. Cat's panties are on the floor as if she had a shower here. And me? I can't remember shit..."

Could it be that Catalina had actually felt sorry for him and came back last night? Yes, that had to be it. She could have put the bottle away and maybe even help him to bed because he would have been too fucked-up to know or remember anything.

Jarod's eyes narrowed, his lips pinched into a thin line. "Okay... so that makes sense right?" he mumbled. But what about the talcum powder? Well maybe he reeked of alcohol and Cat, as nice as she was, had managed to give him a birdbath, finishing it off with her mockingly-favorite Johnson's baby powder.

Right, so far so good. Almost there. It's funny how everything falls into place once you put your mind to it.

And the panties?

Well simple. If he was so fucked-up so that he couldn't even remember getting into bed and so on, how could he remember her getting up, having a shower and heading off to work? And as usual, maybe even to let him know she had been there and that things were back to normal—panties in the hallway.

There you go!

Jarod had to smile at his ingenuity. He felt much better now. Hell! He felt great! What started off as a fucked-up evening ended up a bright and sunny day!

Looked like maybe things were going to be okay after all. And to probably make things even better, he was off work for a little while. And hell... why not? He deserved a break and it would give a chance for him and Cat to patch things up—two birds with one stone.

Jarod picked up the panties and brought it back to his nose for a little whiff. He felt a twinge down under. Cat was back and he couldn't wait to have her home tonight. He would make up for the nights they had missed out together.

He picked himself up and started heading towards the bathroom when he heard his cell phone ring. He headed to the lounge room, thinking he left his phone there last night, but the ring tone was coming from the bedroom. The phone was sitting on the floor, cradled nicely in its charger.

God! Cat has really outdone herself there.

He smiled and picked up the phone.

"Yellowwwwwww," he said cheerfully. "Jarod here!"

"Jarod! Where the fuck are you, dude?" It was James.

Jarod was confused. "What do you mean mate?"

"Well, in case you didn't know, it's now 9:39, and we have a status meeting at 9:45. You forgot?

"Errrr... what? Mate, HR talked to me yesterday. I'm having a month off cause of that bitch Margaret."

"What? What are you talking about? You were here yesterday afternoon! When did this happen?"

Jarod sat down on the edge of the bed. What did James just say? "I was here yesterday? What are you talking about?"

James's voice became impatient. "Hey, listen, I don't have time for this right now. I gotta go dude. Just get your ass over here ASAP, or else HR will really be talking to you."

"Okay, but—"

Before he could finish, the line was dead.

It didn't make any sense. He was sure he was supposed to have a month off. And now James was saying that he had to be in the office? Could it be that they had had a change of heart? Or maybe HR still hadn't informed his section? Anyway, he would sort it out once in the office. So much for the one month's reprieve.

135

Jarod decided to forget the shower. It looked like Catalina had done a good job with the birdbath anyway. He walked to the wardrobe and pulled out a pair of black slacks and a clean white shirt. Somehow the shirt felt different— cleaner, whiter. He shook his head and finished dressing up.

Once at the front door, he pulled out his black shoes from the shoe cabinet. Were they his shoes? They seemed similar but somehow different—cleaner, polished. Nevertheless, he adorned his shoes and opened the front door.

His car was in the driveway. It too seemed cleaner. For the past week, the last thing on his mind would have been to clean his car.

Something didn't add up today.

In fact, many things didn't add up.

Was the shimmer playing tricks on him? Was he starting to lose his mind, to forget simple things? Was this shimmer an onset of Alzheimer?

Jarod got into his cleaner car, took a deep breath, put the key in the ignition and started the engine. It didn't cough and spurt like it normally did. It almost seemed like that the tune up he had kept putting off had finally been done.

With the engine idling quietly like a purring cat, Jarod pulled out of the driveway and pressed on the accelerator. As the car accelerated down the road, he couldn't help but notice how much smoother it felt.

He shook his head.

What the hell is going on?

CHAPTER 19

"**H**i dude," James said. He pulled a cigarette and offered it to Jarod.

"Hi mate." Jarod took the cancer stick and put it between his lips. He lit it up with James's lighter and took a deep drag, letting the welcomed poison fill his lungs —that first one was always the best .

"So what's up with you this morning? You totally missed the status meeting." James took another drag and looked at his cigarette with a frown. "Really gotta stop smoking, dude... this shit's killing us."

"Mate, what are you talking about?" Jarod said." I haven't been at work for a few days already! What the hell is going on?"

James brows came together forming a deep furrow. "What the fuck are *you* talking about?" You were at work yesterday and not only that, but you are the one who arranged this morning's status meeting. The one *you* missed, as a matter of fact."

Jarod leaned against the nearest car—he wasn't feeling so well. First the house, then Catalina who had made an appearance last night, without him remembering squat, the car, and now this.

Jarod felt his head spin and tumbled against the car. He looked as white as a ghost.

James said, "Hey! Are you okay? What's wrong with you?" He quickly took a step forward and caught his friend under the armpit with a claw-like hold.

After a few seconds, color was coming back to Jarod's face. He was still trying to figure out this morning's events and now this. Surprisingly the cigarette was still between his index and forefinger. He brought the half consumed fag to his lips and, his hand shaking, took another drag.

His vision became clearer. "I don't know what's going on mate," he said weakly. His legs began to feel like they might be able to hold his body weight again. "It seems like many things have happened in the last few days—I just don't remember *anything.*"

Still holding his armpit, James pulled out another cigarette, stuck it between his lips and lit it—so much for quitting. A frown appeared on his forehead. "What the hell are you talking about? What do you mean you can't remember anything?"

Jarod squinted and tried trying to recall anything at all—but he couldn't. "I don't know. It's like I keep finding things out since this morning and nothing makes sense. Like, last night I went out with Mary and her grandma and we had dinner and…"

James game him a puzzled look. "Who?"

Jarod didn't have time for this. "Mary," he said. "You know? The kid I told you about, the one I met in the street with her grandma begging."

"Kid? Grandma? Dude, what are you talking about? You have never mentioned anything about a kid or a grandma to me."

A look of despondence masked Jarod's face. "What the fuck, mate? I have! I'm sure I have!" Sweat was now running down from his armpits. He almost wanted to believe that this whole thing was a joke, that James was just having him on, but from the confused look on James' face, he knew it wasn't the case. He knew his friend was dead serious.

Something was definitely wrong.

Jarod wiped the sweat from his forehead and took a deep breath.

James stared at him, bug-eyed. "You are kidding aren't you? You really can't remember anything?"

Jarod's eyes were looking right through James—unblinking. "I don't know anymore, I just don't know. After last night, the bottle of whiskey, I feel like I just woke and...I don't know, everything feels... different."

"Different?"

"There's this blank, this void... like something is missing."

"You got pissed last night?" James took one last drag and flicked his butt on the garage floor.

"Yes, I did. After dinner with...never mind, just after dinner."

James brooded for a few seconds. "Wait a minute, let me get this straight. You apparently had dinner with this Mary and her grandma and, well ,okay, let's just say I forgot you have mentioned them..."

"But I did!" Jarod said defensively.

"Yes, yes, I know, probably I forgot, okay? Let me finish please."

Jarod nodded.

"So, yeah, you had dinner and then you went home, right?"

Jarod smirked guiltily. "Yeah, well, I did have a couple of drinks at the bar before getting home."

"Okay, so you had a couple of drinks at the bar first. And then, you went home and Catalina was there?"

Jarod shook his head. "No, not last night She wasn't there when I got home."

"Okayyyyyy. So then, for whatever reason, you drank a bottle of whiskey?"

Jarod raised his eyes to the sky. "Yes! I needed it. Okay?"

"That's okay mate, that's okay. I'm just trying to understand what happened, not judging."

A car went passed and James looked at it, waiting for it to move on. He rubbed his neck. "So what next, dude? You're basically telling me you woke up this morning and can't remember anything? Not even like anything that happened yesterday?"

Jarod let out a sigh. "Nothing, mate. Well, almost nothing."

James put his hands deep into his pockets, seemingly to avoid the temptation of another cigarette. "What do you mean, *almost* nothing?"

"I remember dinner with Mary and her grandma. I remember my fucked-up life and talking to HR, Cat leaving me, and. the shit that started all this: the shimmer."

James looked totally confused. "The what? Shimmer? What the hell is the shimmer."

Jarod looked up, his eyes narrowing into two tiny slits. "Seriously mate? Now you are going to tell me I have never mentioned the shimmer before?" His voice rose. "You're saying that not only am I forgetting everything, but that I'm also making shit up?"

Beads of sweat started to form high up on Jarod's forehead. He could feel the blood rushing into his cranium like a flood engulfing every little conceivable hideout. His mind started racing as he tried to figure out what was going on in his head. In a way, he knew James wasn't lying—he had no reason to. He knew James did not remember anything about Mary or the shimmer. As impossible as it seemed, he knew something was drastically wrong, and he also knew that *that* something was him.

James looked at his watch and his eye brows shot up. "Shit mate! It's eleven. We need to go back. I have another meeting, like now!"

Jarod opened his mouth but nothing came out.

James put his arm around his shoulder and led him to the elevator.

Jarod didn't want to face work. He didn't want to find out what else he didn't know. But he was in a daze, and he let James guide him into the elevator.

Before he knew it, they were headed for the 28th floor.

His department.

****

The elevator door opened with a clunk. They had used the back delivery elevator with its wide doors and wooden panels interior to make a discreet entrance into the back of the office as if coming back from one of the meeting rooms.

They hadn't said anything in the elevator—both of them were lost in their own thoughts.

Jarod walked ahead of James and headed for his cubicle. He was turning into the little corridor that would lead him there when James grabbed his arm and pulled him back.

"Where are you going dude?" James said, a concerned look on his face.

Jarod looked at him, baffled. "What do you mean, where am I going?" he paused. "My desk mate, where else would I be going?"

This time James looked at Jarod as if he had totally lost it— his jaw dropped. "What the fuck! What is wrong with you today? You've moved to your new office two month ago! You can't even remember that?"

Jarod felt his head spin. Stars started to form in front of his eyes. He could feel a cold sweat emanating from every pore. Shock was replaced by a worried look.

141

James said, "Dude? Are you okay?" His voice seemed distant and faded like a cloud drifting away in the horizon. "Hey dude?"

Jarod could hear the concern. The voice was coming back. He felt James' grip on his arm and the blood came rushing back to his paper-white face, bringing him back to his senses.

Jarod wiped his mouth with his free hand and swiped the sweat from his brow. "I'm okay. I don't know what happened. Just felt dizzy. "

Jarod began to react to what had just happened. It wasn't just last night or yesterday he couldn't remember—it was a whole two fucking months!

James still held on to Jarod's arm and lead him to his unknown office. All eyes were on him.

Then he saw her.

The bitch.

She was sitting at her usual spot. She was also looking at him, but there was no malice. She looked different. The way she was looking at him was different. Was that concern he saw in her eyes? No hate? No sarcasm? No fuck-you-I'm-the-boss look? Just plain, simple worry?

James reached the end of the hallway with Jarod tagging behind him like a lost puppy. He stopped at the entrance and pointed with his chin to the black and white sign on the door. "Remember now?" he said.

Jarod felt bile rise at the back of his throat. He swallowed but still could taste the acidic remains. He felt his hands becoming clammy from the excessive dampness that was building up from deep within his confused soul. He was beyond trying to understand and just force his mind to accept was he was seeing.

The white lettering was starting back at him in defiance.

"JAROD JOHNSON – HEAD OF RISK MANAGEMENT."

CHAPTER 20

Finally seated down, Jarod looked around his office. He couldn't believe it. How did he end up from almost losing his job to being the Head of Risk Management. The whole thing was so crazy. He didn't know what to think—what was happening? He remembered nothing.

Amnesia? Did he hit his head whilst having one-too-many and couldn't recall the last two months? Was he going crazy? Did the shimmer do this? Make him forget everything?

In front of him was a large desk. Behind it he could see two chairs—he guessed he was obviously important enough to receive visitors. There was a terminal facing him and some yellow sticky-notes surround it like flies on shit. He pulled out one of the notes:

REVIEW CACS PROJECT RISK ASSESS/ SIGN-OFF BY FR.

Suddenly, Jarod felt a searing pain as a torrent of information unexpectedly flooded into his hippo-campus—no more than a second of two—and then the pain was gone.

He shook his head and looked at the note again. But this time, somehow, his rewired brain seemed to know what the note was about. He didn't know how he knew—but he did. As if triggered by the note, a new memory had shot into his mind. He put down the note and picked up a folder that was sitting on the desk to his left. It read 'CACS RM PROJ RECON' on the front cover page. He opened it.

His eyes skimmed through the contents. As he read each word, he could feel the same tingling sensation, but less painful now, coming from the center of his brain. Memories surfaced—memories that meant nothing to him to begin with, but memories that somehow were starting to shape and rewrite his past. A past all new to him, yet a past he had already lived.

He frantically opened more folders. His eyes scanned them faster than anyone would have been able to digest the amount of data that was entering his mind. But yet, somehow he recognized the past that had never been. There were handwritten notes and comments he had made. He read them now and they all made sense. They were new memories and old memories at the same time.

Jarod dropped the folders. He sat back on his swivel chair, his mouth agape, his mind overwhelmed by the amount of information it had just absorbed.

He looked around *his* office. Something started to hit him —a realization—*his* notes…but they were not really *his*.

Every time he looked at something, it seemed to trigger a memory. Yet, he knew he had never even set foot in this office, let alone working as the Head of Risk Management. It was almost as if he had stepped into someone else's shoes.

Jarod closed his eyes. He tried to remember. Then without warning, a memory came back. This time, a real memory— one that actually matched his *real* past. Dr. Andrews came into his mind. He remembered how he had said that he may have been able to see another parallel universe through the shimmer.

"No," Jarod said, his tired head resting in his hands. "No! It's impossible!"

He opened his eyes and looked around again. James had said that he had been in the office the day before. Yet, he knew for certain he hadn't been. He didn't want to believe it but it all seemed to be so real. It was like he wasn't just seeing another universe but actually *was* in another universe! A universe where his past was different than the one he remembered—no, the one he had lived. His past had diverged at some point, and his life had followed at different tangent altogether. A new past. A past where he had been successful. A past where he had had a career, and a past where Catalina was still with him.

Now it all made sense.

Him waking-up in bed without a hangover. Catalina's panties on the floor. The missing bottle of whiskey. Even the car that worked perfectly—the car he should have brought to the garage for a tune-up.

Jarod closed his eyes. He rested his elbows on his desktop and put his head in his hands. He was tired—confused.

He knew he was going to wake up. It was all just a bad dream.

"Okay, okay," he said to himself. "I'm going to keep my eyes closed for a minute and then, I'm going to wake up. And as soon as I wake up, everything will be as it should be. I'm gonna have a massive headache, and a hangover to boot, and the house is gonna be empty, and I'm gonna feel like shit. But at least I'll be back where I belong, and this will all just be a bad dream."

He lay his hands back on the desk, his eyes remaining closed. "Okay, right. Here we go, I'm just gonna count to three, and all this will be gone." He leaned back on his chair. "One, two..." he hesitated, not knowing what he would see when he'd open his eyes. "And..." he held back—one more second. "Three!"

Jarod opened his eyes, certain he'd wake up lying in his own vomit, and more than happy to have his face and clothes smeared in the foul stench—but nothing had changed.

Almost nothing.

James was standing at the door with a what-the-fuck-are-you-doing look on his face. "Sup, dude?" he said nonchalant as if he hadn't seen anything.

"Err...was just...daydreaming, mate," Jarod said Jarod nervously, like a kid caught with his hand in the cookie jar. He wondered how long James had been standing there. Should he tell him he couldn't remember squat? By the way his friend had reacted earlier on, he quickly decided against it. James must already think he is crazy and telling him that *he* had just not being *him* the last few weeks of his life didn't seem like the smartest move right now.

The room was swimming. He shook his head, trying to re-stabilize it. His friend was looking at him. A frown creasing his forehead—waiting.

Jarod decided to play the game and keep it to himself, for now anyway. At least until he could figure out what was going on. He looked up at James, played along and pretended nothing had happened.

"Are you okay, dude?" James said settling into one of the guest's chairs. There was concern written all over his face.

"I don't know," Jarod said in a tired voice. The whole thing seemed so crazy and, even if he had wanted to, he wouldn't have known where to start anyhow. "Mate, even if I were to tell you anything, you'd probably think I'm a total nutcase—I'm starting to feel that way."

James leaned back and crossed his long legs under the desk, "Come on, dude, this is me you're taking to. I can see something is wrong with you this morning. You gotta let me in buddy." He uncrossed his legs, leaned forward and lowered his voice. "Listen, whatever it is, I'm here to help you. You're my best friend. You know that, right?"

"I know, mate. I know, and you are also my best friend." Jarod sighed, his mouth forming a thin line. "Honestly, I'm not sure what's wrong. It's like I'm in a dream. I do have an idea, but it sounds so crazy I'd be better off in a loony bin with the keys thrown out."

"Dude, try me, okay? I think you're a total nutcase anyway!" James laughed trying to make light of the situation. "Nothing you could tell me would surprise me!"

Jarod didn't react but just sat there looking lost. "Tell you what mate," he finally said, "let me try to figure it out first, and when I'm sure of what's going on without the risk of ending up in a mental institution, I'll let you know. Okay?"

James got up. "It's cool bro." He reluc-tantly moved towards the door. "You know where to find me, dude..."

James stepped out.

The office was empty again.

All that remained was Jarod, his eyes fixed on the door.

His mind in another world.

CHAPTER 21

Jarod stood at the bottom of the stairs. The dark entrance looked and smelled the same. It felt like walking into a public toilet. If anyone could show him he wasn't going crazy, it would be Mary.

He had left work early and decided to go straight to Mary's home. Now, here he was, and in a few minutes he would know if it was shimmer's doing.

When Jarod reached the front gate of Mary's sub-divided home, he pulled out his cell phone and looked for her number. He scrolled up and down the listing of names—Mary's number was missing. How could that be possible? He felt a bead of sweat forming high up on his brow and trickling down his temple. He looked around, not sure what to do. The dark stairway's stench reached his nostrils—at least that hadn't changed.

He checked his cell phone listing again.

Was it possible he had deleted her number by mistake? He couldn't remember doing so but then, there was a lot he couldn't remember lately. He just stood there—dead silence.

After a minute, he heard a creak behind him and turned around to the see the entrance door to the apartment behind him slightly ajar. He could just see half a face—white hair, deep crisscrossing crevasses that reminding him of a desert that hadn't seen a drop of rain in many years, and a single gray eye.

As soon as Jarod saw her, the door started to close. He took a few hurried steps towards the old woman.

"No! Please, wait!" he cried out in desperation.

But it was too late.

By the time he had reached the door, it was closed. He had to get to Mary—somehow.

He knocked on the door, soft at first and then harder. He knew the old woman was there, probably too afraid to open it. He knocked several more times and realized it wasn't going to happen.

He turned around with a lump in his throat. Maybe if he banged at Mary's gate hard and loud enough, someone might hear him and come out. He dropped his cell phone back into his pocket and banged hard enough for anyone beyond the gate to hear him.

"Mary! Are you there?" He paused for a few seconds and listened—nothing. "Mary! It's Jarod! Hellooo? Mary!"

He kept at it for what seemed like an eternity and finally gave up. Disappointed and feeling the sweat starting to drench his shirt, he turned around, ready to make his way back down the damp stairway.

Then he heard a door being opened from inside the gate. His heart jumped and skipped a beat. He quickly turned and ran back up the three steps that separated him from the gate.

"Mary? Is that you?" he said, his face against the rusted steel bars in a attempt to peer around the bend of the narrow corridor, anticipating Mary's smiling face.

But it wasn't Mary.

The young man who rounded the corner was in his twenties. He was tall and skinny, looking lost in his over-sized tee-shirt that went halfway down to his thighs. The tracksuit pants he was wearing seemed to have once been the home of a family of moths. His young face showed surprise and slight annoyance at seeing Jarod.

The man arrived at the gate but stood back a little unsure. "Can I help you sir?"

The man's English was very good, and Jarod was taken aback. He thought he would have had to start using sign language in order to explain his situation. "Please," he said, "I'm looking for a little girl called Mary. She lives at the end of the hallway. The door to the right; and she lives with an old woman, her grandmother."

The young man looked at him with a crease forming between his dark, narrow eyes. "I'm sorry," he said, "but no Mary or old woman live here."

Had they moved out? Mary would have told him. Maybe she did, maybe he just didn't remember. "Oh, maybe they moved out? I mean, they used to live here, like last week right?"

The young man's narrow eyes became even smaller. He was studying Jarod, seeming to try to figure out who he could be. "No," he said to Jarod's disappointment. "I have lived for a year in this building, and there is no one here by the name of Mary. The people who live next door to me are an old couple —there's no children living here."

Jarod had to hold on to the door. This was not possible. Maybe he had gone to the wrong building? They all looked quite similar after all, there was always that chance. But the smell, the urine, the gate—no, this was definitely the right building. "Are you sure? Maybe you didn't see the young girl? Maybe you missed her."

The young man shook his head. "No, I'm sure, sir. I'm sorry. There is no Mary here. No young girl, just the old couple since I've been here."

Jarod felt his head spin. He stumbled back and his foot found the back wall which stopped him from falling.

"Sir?" the man said, concern in his tone. "Are you okay?" He fumbled for his keys, opened the gate and quickly moved towards Jarod who was now sitting on the filthy floor, his back against the even filthier wall.

The young man's voice was distant. Jarod could barely discern what he was saying.

"Sir? Do you want me to call an ambulance?" He knelt down in front of Jarod and held his wobbly head.

Jarod's eyes were half-closed but he could see the concerned look on the man's face when reality started to resurface. He shook his head and put both hands against the slimy wall behind him. With the young man's help, his legs feeling like spaghetti, he heaved himself back up to a standing position

"I'm sorry," he heard himself say, like it was the right thing to say but somehow it felt like someone else was saying it. "I'm sorry, I just felt a bit dizzy. I'm fine now really. I think I'm in the wrong building." he lied, knowing fairly well that he was in Mary's building.

The young man studied Jarod, his hand still hooked under his armpit. "Are you sure you don't want me to call an ambulance, sir? Or maybe I can get you a glass of water?"

Jarod was coming back. Everything around him was solid now. And the smell was back—that had to be good. His mouth felt like cotton. "That would be good thank you."

He stared at the iron gate while the young man hurriedly stepped through it. He heard his footsteps hurrying down the corridor—the corridor when *once* there had been a little girl with a sweet smile. He tried to get the thought out of his mind. The thought that perhaps there had never been a Mary here. The crazy, *crazy* thought that maybe he didn't just catch a glimpse of a parallel world anymore.

But he had actually *jumped* into one.

CHAPTER 22

He felt the whiskey slowly makes its way down. The warmth hit the pit of his stomach. Well, at least that was one thing that hadn't changed. His closed his eyes and savored the remains of the blended mixture on his tongue.

He opened his eyes again and looked around the room. He noticed some subtle changes—not many, but enough to tell him he wasn't where he was supposed to be. The television seemed to be out of place by a couple of inches. It's been moved to the right. He noticed a picture to the left of it. He was pretty sure it hadn't been there before.

The picture is surrounded by a white iron frame with four hearts—one on each corner. In it he can see a photo of Catalina and him on a beach. It looks like some kind of resort. He has his arm around her waist, and she is wearing a Polka dot bikini. She looks as sexy as ever. He is wearing a pair of cut denims with a plain white tank top. A dark tan covers them both. Behind them he can see a hotel. The hotel has a name on top but he cannot distinguish it from the couch.

He puts his whiskey down by the couch and slowly gets up, his eyes not leaving the picture—every step bringing him closer to the inevitable truth. The words are starting to take shape. When finally he can see them, his mind is trying in vain to reject them. But his eyes, now totally focused on the name, know what they see.

HILTON WAIKIKI BEACH HOTEL

Jarod cannot feel his legs anymore, it's like they've been cut right under him. His body, as if boneless, slowly crumbles under its own weight. He is lying in the carpet, his head turned toward the picture, his eyes never leaving it even as his body has already given up trying to hold him.

Jarod knows he has never been to Hawaii.

He tries to lift a hand to wipe the tear he can feel flowing from the corner of his right eye. He cannot move a muscle. He feels paralyzed by the undeniable truth.

A sharp pain, deep inside his head.

He can almost feel the neurotransmitters diffuse across the spaces between his cells, making bridges to neighboring cells, creating new memories. Recollections that are new to him now feel every gap—reminiscence of another life. His brain starts to fill up with images of the trip that never was. The trip to Hawaii. Catalina, so happy. The beach, the sunset, the love making under the stars. The picture, taken by the friendly driver, in front of the Hilton.

It's all there. Taking shape in his head, like a film he is seeing for the first time, yet a film he has relived a thousand times before.

Within a minute, the whole trip has flooded in, like it has always belonged there, inside his head. There were no more doubts in Jarod's mind—he *had* been there. Every moment of that trip was now sitting in his hippo-campus. His brain had instantly rewired itself. New connections had been created between his brain cells, forming new memories triggered by the simple act of having had a look at the picture next to the television set.

****

It was all clear to him now. He finally realized what was happening. He knew he wasn't where he was supposed to be. The shimmer had done this—he was sure of it.

Jarod stood on his elbow. His head was spinning but he was able to make his way back to the couch. His hand absently picked up the whiskey—the ice cubes have now merged with the alcohol. The diluted liquid was a welcomed relief to his racing mind. He tried to remember the events from the day before. The dinner with Mary and Pawpaw. Getting drunk. Passing out. Waking up.

That was it.

He had woken up that morning, and that was when it had all started. That was the time he had noticed something was wrong. First the missing bottle of whiskey, then he should have had a hangover but there hadn't been a trace of it. Catalina's panties by the bathroom door. And James. Yes, James who had called him to come to work. And finally, not only did he have a job but he had been promoted to Head of Risk Management. And Mary, yes, Mary. Who had never existed...

And the memories.

The memories that have been flooding in — triggered by him simply looking at an object—a note, a photograph. It was all so obvious to him now. Doctor Andrews had been right. He had been able to see a parallel world through the shimmer, but that hadn't been it—that hadn't been *all*. Jarod now knew that he had somehow jumped into this other universe. A portal had been opened to him, and he had gone right through it.

The images.

The legs that Mary and him had been able to see. They had been able to take a glimpse into another reality—an untouchable reality, until now.

Everything was real.

All the universes were real.

Together they existed, heading in different directions in an never-ending web of life, spreading their fingers to every uncharted corner, creating new beginnings... new chances... new Jarods.

EPILOGUE

Many years had gone past and Jarod had accepted his new life. There was no point denying it or even trying to understand what had happened. His new life had been good to him, and most of it was probably due to the shimmer being but a distant nightmare.

He had ended up marrying Catalina and his career had flourished to a director position. His brain had been rewired. New connections had been formed, triggered by new experiences and things he had seen or heard. People he had never met had come into his life seamlessly. He had played the game of pretending to know who they were until enough memories had formed in his brain for him to really remember.

Jarod was settled in his favorite couch. He loved this couch —it held many memories, both old and new. They had moved three times since they had gotten married on that beautiful summer day, and every time she had wanted to get rid of it. But Jarod couldn't do it. The couch represented the one link he had with his former life. The only link that could really remind him of whom he really was and where he came from.

He took a sip of his whiskey. "Some habits never die," he said to himself. He tended to do that more often as the years had gone by, maybe just to make sure *he* was still *him*. "No matter where you might end up…"

He looked around the room and smiled at the thought of his now-wrinkled face surrounded by a halo of thin, white hair.

Next to the television set, as it had always been since the first day he had laid eyes on it, was the picture. Catalina and him still looked young and beautiful standing in front of the Hilton, so many years ago, although Jarod couldn't deny that at sixty-two, his wife was still as beautiful to him as the first day he had seen her across the bar, sipping on her martini.

Another thought came to his mind and his smile widened. Just like his couch and his whiskey, some things have never changed. Things that had been there in his former world and things that were there now—as if, they too, had managed to cross over—Catalina's panties. Surprisingly, she still wore sexy, silk panties, even at her ripe old age. And surprisingly they were still dropped by the bathroom door every-time she stepped into the shower. And once in a while, she would turn her head towards him, knowing very well that he would be looking, and she would give him that mischievous smile with that sparkle in her eyes. This would often have him stepping into the bathroom to make love to her—right there on the bathroom floor, like two teenagers.

Jarod swallowed the remainder of his whiskey and headed towards the kitchen. He put the glass into the sink and the bottle on the highest kitchen shelf. Not that that had ever done much good anyway.

Catalina was visiting her old friend Sophie. They had stayed in touch over these years, and Sophie, true to her word, had never gotten married. She had become very successful and totally enjoyed her life, as she always had.

Jarod decided to go for a walk—he didn't want to stay home alone. He had always enjoyed the outdoors and wasn't much of an indoor person.

The weather was a bit cool so he decided to put on his coat. Where could he go? There was an old local coffee shop not too far, one that had managed to survive despite the ever growing competition that sprouted at every corner like mushrooms in the damp niche of an old elm tree.

Heading out the door, Jarod made his way across the street. It was Monday and the usual crowds were already sitting inside their cubicles. He looked at the people going past him. It was funny, he thought, that as you got older you took time to observe and reflect—see things that you would never have noticed during your youth when life had you by the balls. and you were constantly lost in your own thoughts.

Upon reaching the street corner, Jarod turned left. Already he could smell the aroma of the coffee that was still two hundred yards away, and his nostril flared in response.

Suddenly, something caught he eyes just as he was passing the 7-Eleven. An old woman was sitting against the wall. She was old. Very old. Wrinkles lined her face like the severely cracked soil of a desert that hadn't seen rain for a hundred years. The eyes had formed cataracts that veiled them as if her light brown irises were trying to hide behind the milky substance. Her hair, gray and streaked with white, were pulled back into a bun that was too tight and seemed to want to stretched the skin around her temple to make her brow seem smoother. Her tiny nose was like a button that was placed there just for the hell of it. Her aged cracked lips framed crooked yellow teeth that were held together by a single wire with gaps wide enough to leave little to the imagination as to the inside of her mouth. Her clothes were ragged but clean. Everything she wore was black or gray, and it was almost as if all the colors had been drained from her presence, just like in a one-hundred-year old photograph. Her cardigan was moth-eaten in several places, and the black trousers she was wearing were held together by a length of cord coiled around her thin frame. To her left sat an old cookie steel box that looked like it hadn't seen a crumb in fifty years. A few coins were sitting inside it.

Jarod felt his head spin a little. His hand shot out and the wall beside him saved him from his legs giving way under him. A very, very distant memory, trapped in an old recess of his mind sprang up—Pawpaw.

The old woman looked up at Jarod. She attempted a smile that showed crooked, yellow teeth. She extended a shaky hand, which looked more like a claw, and Jarod found his own hand, as if it had a mind of its own, searching deep into his pocket, looking for some loose change.

Never leaving her eyes, he felt a couple of coins, but just as he started digging them out, he saw a white gloved hand dropping a fifty dollar note into the old woman's extended claw. Jarod let the coins drop back into the depth of his pocket, feeling his face heating up with guilt at what he had thought was a generous jest.

He reached for his wallet.

His eyes left the old woman's white, veiled eyes, as they had left his, and were now concentrated on the stranger who had deposited the fifty dollar note into her hand.

The body attached to the fifty dollar bill was wiry, but the expensive coat it was adorned with made the owner look distinguished, even though Jarod had not as yet seen her face.

Finally, his eyes set upon the owner's face. It was slightly turned towards the old woman. Her hair were dark and parted in the middle like a path dividing a field, and were kept neat but long enough to reach her slender shoulders. Upon her small nose sat a pair of Ray Band, black, framed glasses that gave her a distinguished look, even-though there were slightly too big for her slight Asian face.

Then Jarod saw it.

It was almost indistinguishable but there nevertheless. Like a flashback, he saw his whole life, the old and the new, flood back into his head. Catalina, the whiskey, Pawpaw, the shimmer....Mary.

Mary.

The small thin scar running from her bottom lip down to the corner of her chin.

Jarod took an involuntary step back—almost losing his balance. The woman turned towards him and their eyes met. Jarod's mind was racing. He opened his mouth, not really knowing what would come out. "Mary?"

The woman's dark eyes—almost too big for her small face —squinted into two narrow slits. Jarod saw confusion in them. It seemed her mind was trying to make sense of what *she* was seeing.

****

It seems like a lifetime ago, and it a way, it is. She wasn't crazy after all.

She remembers. It's been decades but she has never forgotten her previous life.

"Jarod?" was all Mary could mutter.

www.ingramcontent.com/pod-product-compliance
Lightning Source LLC
Chambersburg PA
CBHW020129180626
46810CB00004B/1476